A Castle for Christmas

A Castle for Christmas

The Back Inn Time Series

Book Four

Stephenia H. McGee

By The
Vine Press

Cover design: Roseanna White Designs
Cover model: Collins Doster
Model photography: Period Stock, LLC
Other images used under license from Shutterstock.com.

Library Cataloging Data
Names: McGee, Stephenia H. (Stephenia H. McGee) 1983 –
Title: A Colonial Courtship / Stephenia H. McGee
234p. 5 in. × 8 in.
Description: By The Vine Press digital eBook edition | By The Vine
Press Trade paperback edition | Mississippi: By The Vine Press, 2021
Summary: A crown meant for a princess. A medieval castle. And a one-
way ticket to an unforgettable romance.
Identifiers: ISBN-13: 978-1-63564-062-5 (trade) | 978-1-63564-061-8
(ebk.)
1. Christian Fiction 2. Time Travel Romance 3. Historical Romance 4.
Clean and Wholesome Romance 5. Time Travel 6. Religious Fiction 7.
Inspirational Romance

Dear reader,

As a historical fiction writer, I've always wondered what it would be like if I could travel back in time and get a firsthand glimpse of the eras I love to read about. Thus, the idea for this series was born. It's a fun way to imagine the impossible.

Please keep in mind, dear reader, that a *story* is all this is meant to be. It is not meant to spark a theological debate on whether God would allow the miracle of time travel. The Bible tells us "Man's days are determined; You [God] have decreed the number of his months and have set limits he cannot exceed" (Job 14:5) and "My times are in your hands" (Psalm 31:15).

Several of the things regarding the time travel in this story are not possible, but it allows us to suspend what we know to be true to simply enjoy the fictional freedom of the *what if...?* So, come with me, imaginative reader, and together let's go see what it might be like to "step back *inn* time and leave our troubles behind"!

Happy reading!
Stephenia

One

The best part of dying was that she got to eat whatever she wanted. A gal had to count her blessings where she could find them. Avery licked the chocolate from her finger and crumpled the little white bag that had held the decadent éclair. She checked her face in the car's rearview mirror. None of her donut-for-dinner meal clung to her skin.

The new makeup looked pretty good, effectively hiding the dark rings under her eyes. No sense giving strangers any clues to her struggles. She was here to celebrate, after all. Alone and not at all where she'd expected to be, but she wouldn't let such details derail her. Avery pulled her suitcase from the rental car's trunk and locked the doors.

A grand Victorian stood like a genteel lady wrapped in sunset colors, the edges of her cloak dappled in the deep purple of evening. A cool ocean breeze tickled Avery's senses, slipping past the bare branches of ancient oaks that hid the Gulf of Mexico from view.

What a stunning house. Avery paused at the sign, contemplating a selfie. But why bother? Only a few acquaintances at work would see the picture, and they thought she was on a little bit of… well, a *less permanent* vacation. Avery left the phone in her pocket, determined not to let melancholy thoughts rob her of her "last month as a sane person" adventure.

The sprawling Victorian house nestled in the quaint seaside town hadn't been on her itinerary. Giving into spontaneous whims, however, had kind of become her thing. She smiled at the motto on the sign. *Step back inn time and leave your troubles behind.*

If only life were that simple.

Avery pulled the wobbly suitcase behind her and mounted the steps to a pristine wrap-around porch boasting an abundance of Christmas decorations. Poinsettias lined the railing, candles with dancing flames dotted the wide windows, and a wreath with a spray of greenery, festive ribbons, and sparkling ornaments graced the front door.

She lifted her hand to knock just as the door swung open. A woman with graying curls and a bright smile greeted her.

"Hello, Miss Stuart." The woman gestured her inside. "I've been waiting for you. Do come in."

Avery stepped into a front room that looked like something from a Hallmark movie. Every doorway dripped in garland. Every tabletop boasted a manger scene, glass tree, or shiny knickknack. At least she wouldn't be spending Christmas somewhere lacking character.

"This way, dear. I have cookies in the kitchen."

Avery followed the woman around a massive staircase, past several antique rooms, and to a wide kitchen every bit as elegant as she'd come to expect from the graceful Victorian.

"I hope you like snickerdoodles." The woman plucked a plate from a granite countertop and extended it in Avery's direction.

The suitcase behind her clinked over the tiled floor as Avery drew closer. "Thank you, Miss...uh...?"

"Silly me." The woman set the plate back on the counter. "I'm Mrs. Easley." Instead of offering her hand, the woman dropped into what Avery could only call the most perfect debutant curtsy she'd ever seen.

"Oh...I, uh." Avery positioned the suitcase upright. "Nice to meet you. I'm Avery." She clutched the suitcase handle. Sticking her hand out now would be awkward. Even more so than stating her name to someone who already knew it. Though probably not any more awkward than a middle-aged woman curtsying in a pair of black slacks and a gaudy Christmas sweater. The kind with blinking lights.

"I'm so glad you'll be joining us." Mrs. Easley bustled over to the long counter positioned opposite a row of enchanting windows that would likely bathe the space in golden light come morning. She plucked a massive old book from a built-in shelf and plopped it onto the center island.

Avery eyed the cookies. Should she grab one, or wait for the lady to offer again? Sure, she'd just finished an éclair, but these smelled amazing.

Mrs. Easley flopped open the front cover of the book and scanned what appeared to be a table of contents. "Let's see…December." She ran her finger down a line. "Ah. Here we are." She flipped to a page a few chapters in. "Miss Avery Stuart." A slight frown dipped her cheery lips as she paused, reading something.

Sympathetic eyes glanced up for only a moment, then returned to the page. What in the world was in that book?

Mrs. Easley closed the cover gently. "You get the tower room, my dear."

The tower room?

"It is my favorite, you see." The words were soft. The same kind of soft that had come from Doctor Flynn. A smile stretched the older woman's lips. "From up there you can see the ocean."

Then why did the lady sound so sad? Before she could ask, Mrs. Easley scooped up the plate of cookies and shooed Avery out of the kitchen. "Would you like a tour?"

"Sure." She followed behind her flighty hostess, soaking up the beauty of the house. "This is a very pretty place. I'm lucky to have stumbled across your website."

"No such thing as luck, dear girl. You're exactly where you need to be."

Avery withheld comment as Mrs. Easley showed her around the bottom floor, which consisted of a parlor, a library, an office, what appeared to be some kind of ballroom, and a massive dining room. All while still balancing a tray of cookies on one palm. Avery smothered a chuckle at Mrs. Easley's eccentricities. At least Christmas would be interesting with such unique company.

"Will breakfast be served here?" Avery ran her eyes over the bounty of glittering decorations down the center of the table in the dining room.

"That's usually where we eat, yes." The answer had the oddest tinge of evasiveness to it.

"Do you have many guests today?" A house full of people would go a long way to making her feel less lonesome. Even if they were all strangers. Maybe she could organize a mixer. She pushed the thought aside. No. She was on vacation. No jumping back into the party-planning job she'd left behind in Savannah.

Mrs. Easley paused at the doorway leading back out of the dining room. "Not today, dear. Today is for you." She turned away before Avery could come up with a suitable response.

For her? Did that mean no one else would be staying? While a small-town Christmas had a nostalgic ring to it, she didn't fancy spending the holiday in a big house alone.

She was starting to think the woman more than a tad eccentric. The lack of guests three days before Christmas wasn't exactly surprising, however. People had families to visit, parties to attend. Not many would be wandering around aimlessly on their own this time of year.

Not that she would wish her fate on anyone simply so she could have company.

Mrs. Easley led her up a winding staircase to the first landing overlooking the grand entryway. Even this small space held a multitude of decorations. "This is the main floor. Most of our guest rooms are located here." She waved an arm down a long hallway dotted with wall sconces. Up here, Avery could get a feel for what the sign outside had meant. She could almost picture herself having stepped back a century. Even the air felt different.

But that was probably just her senses going haywire again.

At the top of another set of stairs, this one far smaller and enclosed on either side by tight walls that nearly made her feel claustrophobic, they came to a heavy wooden door, the only one on this floor, apparently. This room, unlike the others, had no metal number. Mrs. Easley fished in her pocket and drew out a key. She hesitated a moment, then pulled in a deep breath before sliding the long metal rod into the lock. The door creaked open.

An odd sensation washed over Avery, causing her skin to tingle. The feeling was gone in an instant. Was the unusual sensation another one of the symptoms that had been popping up lately? The doctor hadn't been able to say which ones she'd be most likely to suffer in the coming months.

Mrs. Easley produced a match from somewhere and lit a lantern on the table, then two more on the walls. She turned the wicks, and light reflected off shiny mirrors behind the flames to illuminate the space in warm hues.

She didn't have any electricity up here? That might be a little further "back inn time" than Avery wanted to go. At least it didn't feel cold. If she'd been given a room without heat, she'd find the next Best Western and be on her way.

"The tower room." Mrs. Easley motioned in a sweeping gesture.

A massive bed took up a large hunk of the space, the canopy overhead draped with heavy curtains. A small writing desk, a dresser, a large wingback chair, and a stand with a washbasin completed the furnishings. Three massive windows overlooked the front yard, their frames holding wispy lace sheers. Beyond the delicate curtains, twilight touched the ripple of waves just visible over the tops of the trees.

Mrs. Easley pointed to a door tucked in one corner. "We added a small bath some years ago. It's not big, but it gets the job done." Her gaze dropped to the platter of cookies she still carried as though just now remembering them. "Oh, yes. These are for you." She deposited the plate on the writing desk and ran a hand down her sweater.

The room was nice, if a bit antiquated. The lack of lighting, however, had Avery concerned. She slipped her cell from the back pocket of her jeans. "Thanks." She toyed with her phone. She hadn't paid anything yet. She could probably still find another room. But then, she was feeling pretty drained. One night couldn't hurt.

"Is there anything you'd like for the evening?" Mrs. Easley glanced around, seeming oddly reluctant to leave. "Anything special I can do for you?"

Avery tapped a finger on the handle of her suitcase. "I might ride around and look at some Christmas lights later. If I'm not too tired. Any place you recommend?"

"Downtown has a beautiful display." Mrs. Easley checked her watch. "Anything you'd like me to cook?"

The plate of cookies would do. "No, thanks. I'm good."

The woman hesitated in the doorway. "What about music? A book maybe? How about a movie? I can bring up the television."

Smiling, Avery shook her head. The woman was

kind. "All good. I'll let you know if I think of anything."

Mrs. Easley nodded, the lines around her mouth serious. "You do that, dear. I mean it." She hesitated only a moment longer. "Well, then. I suppose this is it. Good night."

Avery bid the woman a good night and plopped her suitcase on the desk next to the cookies. An entire platter. Just for her. How sweet. She's stay one night. There would be more rooms somewhere else tomorrow if she wanted to keep moving. She unzipped the top pocket of her suitcase and withdrew her favorite picture. She pressed a kiss to her fingertips, then gently touched the smiling faces of her parents frozen behind timeless glass.

"Pretty place, isn't it?" She set the framed photograph on the desk. Mom would love it here. The thought brought an immediate ache to her chest, sharp pangs of longing squeezing her heart. She dabbed a trickle of moisture from the corner of her eye before plastering on a smile. "What do you think if we stay here through Christmas, then continue to make our way out west? Should be able to hit the slopes by New Year's."

Mind made, she unpacked enough clothes for a three-night stay into the dresser and then looked around. That hadn't taken long. Maybe she should head out and go see the lights. The delectable scent of cinnamon and sugar tickled her senses. But first she'd need a drink to go with her cookies. Snickerdoodles were her favorite, and the extra sugar would give her a boost.

Avery wound her way back downstairs and to the kitchen, where she found the large book still sitting on the counter. Curious, she opened the hefty hardcover. The inside cover had the look of aged wallpaper with a swirling design, and the pages inside were thick and textured.

She flipped to the first page.

Then the next.

Frowning, she lifted a chunk of pages and thumbed through them.

Blank. Every one.

Weird. She plucked a bottle of water from the fridge, hoping Mrs. Easley wouldn't mind. While she sipped it, she eyed the book, not sure which of the two of them might be crazy. She hesitated a moment longer, then made her way back upstairs. The woman was quirky. The show with the book was probably just some prop for the benefit of guests. Something to do with the historical feel of the place.

In any event, Avery didn't get a creepy vibe. At least, not yet. Maybe she'd skip the cookies, though. Just in case. By the time she reached the tower room, her head had started to pound.

So much for the Christmas lights. Maybe she'd do that tomorrow. She'd done enough driving for today, anyway. Comfy pajamas and a Christmas rom-com were exactly what the doctor ordered.

More or less.

How did she find Mrs. Easley to request that TV? She pulled a sappy romance DVD from her suitcase and dropped it on the bed. Maybe Mrs. Easley had a Blu-ray player for her old favorite. If not, this place should at least have Netflix or cable. She'd head down to ask in a minute. Pajamas first.

She was crossing the room when she paused to examine a large drawing that hung on the wall. The center section contained a hand-drawn map, depicting the region of Kent, England. Avery looked closer, the tiny lines of script and old-style drawings reeling her in. Leeds Castle, several manor houses, and a scattering of small villages were all marked with tight, flowing letters. A line of family crests in various designs decorated the bottom.

Huh.

Along both sides of the map, lines of genealogy stretched from the top to the bottom of the poster-sized framed drawing. The left side mapped the lineage of English royalty. About halfway down, a star stood out by one of the names. A matching star stood on the right. Avery moved her attention to the other side of the map.

"Sir Robert de Northwood," Avery read aloud. "Barons. A whole line of them." Her eyes snagged on one line. "Whoa. That's cool."

She put her finger to the place where the name of the fourth Baron of Northwood was written with two little lines connecting it to another name. Lady Avery, foreign princess.

"Well, look at that." Avery winked at the picture of her parents. "Did you know I share a name with a princess from some faraway land?"

Her cheerful voice faded, and silence settled heavily on the room. She knew talking to a photograph made her a bit crazy. But she couldn't give up the last fragment of connection with her parents.

A well of sadness rose within her, and she had to force it back, replacing it with the happiness of fond memories. Her childhood had been marked with princess dresses, tiaras, and tea parties. Avery cast another look at the faces of the people who'd loved her so well. What she wouldn't give to spend this last Christmas with them. She brushed a tear from her eye and got ready for bed.

She paused to look over the names once more, drawing her finger along the lines. "I wonder what you were like, Mr. Baron of Northwood." A fuzzy feeling suddenly overcame her, and Avery took a step back.

Her senses swam. Was dizziness a new symptom? Would she be forced to deal with this as well as the headaches? Holding a hand to her head, Avery stumbled to bed and stretched out on the covers. A moment later, everything went black.

A cool breeze tickled over her face, nudging Avery out of her slumber. She probed her fingers along her temple, but the headache had dissipated as quickly as it had appeared. Goodness. That had been weird. Strange sensations converged upon her senses. Cold, damp air. Something hard beneath her.

Her eyes popped open, revealing a vast sky painted in sunset colors. She sat up. What in the world?

She'd been lying on a hard bench, situated in a well-manicured garden. Had she been sleepwalking? Was that a symptom now too? She swung her feet over the edge, surprised to discover she was wearing an elaborate gown.

Transfixed, she ran her fingers over golden embroidery that created sparkling flowers on the turquoise-and-gold fabric. She stood, turning slightly. The skirt was wide, bellowing out from a narrow waist to completely hide her feet. The bodice fit perfectly, hugging her curves and draping across her neckline. Delicate lace dripped over her shoulders, creating enchanting cap sleeves in the same turquoise. The color scheme reminded her of a mermaid, or perhaps a peacock feather. Something heavy hung from her neck, and she toyed with a necklace. Large gems fell like water droplets from a golden chain, covering her collar bone in a display of sparkling decadence.

Curious, her fingers lifted to her ears, where what she assumed to be matching jewels hung. Her long blond hair tickled the top of her bare shoulders. She touched it gently and discovered what felt like an elaborate twist of curls.

Oh wow. On top of her head sat a crown. The fancy kind with lots of points all around the top and an abundance of jewels.

"What in the world?" Avery stood, turning in her massive princess gown.

Realization dawned. Of course. She'd gone to bed thinking about her father and her childhood days playing king and princess. She giggled.

Never had a dream felt so real. The cold air played along her skin, and she rubbed her hands down her arms. This was awesome. As far as dreams went, she couldn't ask for a better one. Maybe vivid dreams could actually be a good side effect of her brain condition. She craned her neck, looking past the bushes she just now realized were dusted in snow.

Behind them, a massive stone wall rose. She tilted her head back, following it up, up, up.

A castle.

Perfect. This was going to be fun. She lifted her skirt and made her way out of the secluded garden spot, looking for the front door. Maybe Dad would even be here, decked out in royal finery. And Mom would be wearing a gown even more beautiful than Avery's own. The thought had her hurrying forward and bursting out of a hedge wall.

Wow. Old-fashioned carriages stood in a line, their wheels slowly rolling along a gravel drive. Lanterns hung from each one, giant fireflies swinging against the descending twilight. Smells of horses drifted on the air. Avery made her way past three carriages, all with curtains drawn over the windows. She craned her neck to where another large wall enclosed the open area in front of what looked to be the main castle entrance. After a black carriage passed through the gate, a metal portcullis lowered with a grinding screech.

The castle regained her attention. It looked like something from a storybook. But then, why wouldn't it? Turrets and towers and tiny slit windows. Her imagination had gone into overdrive.

"Lady?" A man in a tunic and pair of leggings with knee-high boots approached from around the curve of carriages, a long cloak swirling behind him. He looked from Avery to the last carriage in the line and back again. He frowned. "Is something amiss?"

"Amiss?" Avery laughed. "What could possibly be amiss?"

Men and women in medieval costumes stepped out of the carriages, and knights—the kind in full armor—stood guard. Wow. A few of the costumed people noticed her, their faces openly surprised.

"My lady?" The man's mouth puckered, but he took in her attire and lowered into a bow. "Where is your escort?"

Avery bounced on her toes, excitement bubbling through her veins. "Don't have one." Where was Dad?

"May I offer my service?" The man extended his arm, his narrow face and sharp eyes watching her intently.

Right. She really should be playing the part. Avery tilted her head, doing her best to act the princess. She lifted her eyebrows questioningly. "And who do I have the pleasure of addressing?"

The man drew back as though realizing he'd made some slip in propriety. "Forgive me, my lady. I am Wilhelm. The lord's steward." He bowed again. "My apologies." He cast another look around, clearly dismayed. "May I ask where your retinue has gone?" He checked the line of carriages again, but the last had been emptied of guests and started to roll away.

Avery waved a dismissive hand. "They dropped me off and left." That sounded better than saying she'd woken up in the garden, even though she didn't have to defend herself to a dream man. She rubbed her arms again. She didn't think she'd ever felt so cold in a dream before. How odd. Gravel crunched as the last carriage rolled away, disappearing behind the curve of the castle wall. The people had all gone inside, save for several of the knights, who took positions around the door.

"Please, my lady." The tall man shifted, obviously nervous. What was with this guy? "Allow me to escort you inside before you catch a chill."

Seeing as how she *was* rather interested in viewing the interior of the castle, Avery placed her hand on top of the man's extended elbow in a perfect princess kind of way.

The lanky man guided her toward the stairs leading to the main castle structure enclosed within the wall. "May I ask if you have come for the baron's festivities, milady?"

Festivities? Like a ball? Excitement surged through her. Perfect. "Why, of course I have. I'm rather excited to attend a baron's ball."

Wilhelm cast a glance at her, something in his gaze appraising. "And your name, if I may be so bold as to ask, milady?"

All this "my lady" stuff reminded her of her childhood games. If she was going to have an amazing princess dream, then she might as well make the most of it. She straightened herself to her most regal bearing. "I am Princess Avery of the Kingdom of Gardenia."

The man's footsteps faltered. "I'm unfamiliar with this kingdom. Is it on the continent?"

"It's quite far. I've traveled a great distance to meet your baron. I do so hope he doesn't disappoint."

The man drew back his thin shoulders. "I am certain his lordship will be most interested in meeting you as well." His gaze darted to the crown on her head. "Your Highness."

Avery placed her fingers over her lips to contain a laugh. Oh, yes. This was going to be fun.

Two

"My lord, I must speak to you."

Sir Robert ignored his steward, keeping his attention on the parade of dainty and colorful dresses coming into his great hall. He had to admit, Wilhelm had done a fine job of gathering a collection of potential brides. Ladies in their finest clothing stepped through the archway into the room as Northwood's herald called out each one's title. Robert exhaled a breath of relief. There were now enough guests to fill the tables crowding the hall and leave none of the feast to go to waste.

An expense that would be worth the sacrifice, he reminded himself yet again. Certainly he would secure a match this night. His fingers tightened around the great seal ring on his finger, his now that he had become the lone male member of his family. He must bear the responsibility of providing for his people, even if doing so meant he had to entertain nobles and nearly empty the last of his larders.

"My lord?" Wilhelm stepped closer, still demanding attention. "'Tis of great importance."

Sir Robert turned from his secluded place in an alcove behind the raised dais, trying not to be annoyed with the man for his intrusion. "I will greet them all, Wilhelm. As I said I would."

"Yes, lord. But there is something else."

Whatever Wilhelm had to say, it could wait. Robert wanted to get a look at each woman as she entered the hall before he must make his presence known. By his count, not one of the ladies who'd entered thus far would bring enough to a marriage to undo the damage weighing on Northwood Manor. Not unless Lord Wirth would accept the invitation.

The herald opened his mouth, then paused and turned around to look behind him. Sir Robert leaned forward. Lord Wirth?

"My lord—"

Robert held up a hand, cutting off the steward's words. What had caused the herald to act thusly?

The portly man turned back to the room, clearly startled. He squared his shoulders and his voice projected through the room. "Her Majesty, Princess Avery, of the Kingdom of Gardenia."

The room quieted with the herald's announcement for only a breath, then buzzing whispers spouted across the great hall. Robert pushed off the wall. Royalty. In his castle.

"Why was I not apprised of this?"

Wilhelm sputtered. "I…I have been trying, my lord." Irritation edged into his voice.

Robert pinned him with a look. Apparently, he should have let the man have his say. "Out with it."

"We were not expecting her, my lord. The lady claims to have arrived here on her own." Wilhelm clasped his hands in that way he did whenever he needed to speak of something Robert would not like. "She had no carriage. My education isn't vast my lord, but I haven't heard of this kingdom. Her highness didn't offer much information. I presented her at the door and came to you straightaway."

Wilhelm's words came out in such a jumbled rush that Robert barely caught them all. He grunted and lifted a hand to quiet the man. "Did she say why she'd come?"

"To meet you, my lord. I can only surmise she's arriving as one of the ladies to be selected."

Robert frowned. "What need would a princess have of a baron? Her father would most surely seek a better match."

"I do not know, my lord."

The lady in question slowly entered his hall with the regal bearing befitting her station. Robert's hand tightened around his sword hilt. Royalty at Northwood. Did King Edward know? He stood as transfixed as every other noble in the hall, watching as the lady glided into the room.

She wore a gown like none he'd ever seen. The neckline dropped dangerously low, revealing smooth shoulders. Only a tiny swath of material draped her upper arm, leaving the skin to her fingertips revealed. Robert stepped out of the shadows and started across the hall, the crowd immediately parting in front of him in a swirl of whispers.

The princess paused, her eyes snagging on him. Boldly, she looked at him in such a fashion that his insides tightened. No lady had ever gazed upon him so forthrightly.

Did she find him lacking? Under Wilhelm's assistance, he'd taken care to bathe and groom for the night's events. Warm, honey-brown eyes slid over him, and then a small smile broke the serenity of graceful features.

It took more of his training than he would admit to keep his gaze steady and his steps secure. The woman was mesmerizing. Like something from a bard's fables. Wholly unlike any lady he'd seen before. Not that he'd spent much time in court. He'd seen royalty in passing when he'd been a lad at Leeds Castle, but none of them had been of a kind with the creature before him.

Sir Robert bowed, aware that every set of eyes in the hall had landed on him. "Your Highness. Welcome to my home. I am Sir Robert, Baron of Northwood."

The lady smiled as though she knew something he

did not, then dipped into a deep curtsy.

Only then did he notice the jewels. He'd been so focused on her features and the daring cut of her gown that he'd missed the elaborate crown nestled in a heap of shimmering curls, not a single lock hidden beneath a proper veil. The Kingdom of Gardenia must be prosperous. An advantageous match, to be sure. Though highly suspect.

"If I may ask, Your Highness." Robert bowed deeply. "What brings you to Northwood?"

She laughed lightly, her gaze flitting around the room like a butterfly. "I heard there was a ball."

Had she come to seek a match, as Wilhelm implied? "We are most honored to receive you." He straightened. "Northwood is at your service."

"Thank you, Baron. I'm most grateful for your hospitality."

He gave a curt nod, not entirely sure what to make of the woman before him. She spoke strangely, with a lilt to her words he could not place.

He had not been of a mind to host such an event in the first place and would not have, if not for the dire needs of his people. If he hoped to help them through the winter, he would have to refill the empty coffers his brother had left him. That, and his sister's profound insistence upon an heir, had convinced him. A mission left to her by their mother, no doubt.

The princess watched him a moment. "So, will there

be dancing?"

Dancing? He looked to Wilhelm, who had apparently followed him across the room and now stood awkwardly at his side. At Wilhelm's slight nod, Robert addressed the princess. "Dancing. Certainly, Your Highness. If you wish it." The castle had minstrels, though he'd planned for them to play while he made his rounds with the noblemen. But, if royalty wished for dancing, then there would be dancing.

She clasped long fingers together. "Who wouldn't wish dancing at a ball?" She surveyed the room before turning expectant eyes on him.

"I will see the hall prepared after the meal is completed."

The smile she flashed his way sent strange energy through him. The kind he'd only experienced when being spotted by the stag he hunted or preparing for battle. The foreign princess had set his senses on edge.

"You use our language well, highness. Do they speak Anglo-French in your kingdom?"

"Anglo...?" She pressed her fingers to her lips. "Interesting. I thought I only spoke English." She shrugged as though she hadn't just said something entirely peculiar.

Robert shared a look with Wilhelm. Perhaps the princess was lacking in wits. Robert gestured toward the dais, past the swarm of nobility pretending not to scrutinize them. "Would her highness care to join me at the high table?"

"I would be delighted, Baron. Thank you."

The crowd parted for them, and he extended his arm to help her up the single step to the raised platform, where he pulled out a chair for her to his left. He sat next to her, surprised to find Wirth on his right. How had he missed the baron's arrival? The graying man had indeed come with his daughter, a lady with a sizable dowry that would go a long way to righting the state of Northwood. Sir Alfred de Wirth's attendance had been Robert's greatest hope prior to the unexpected guest's arrival.

Despite knowing the lady de Wirth to be his most likely match, however, he couldn't pull his attention from the strange foreign princess. A malady, he noted, glancing around, that the guests in the hall shared. As such, perhaps Wirth would forgive him.

"Is this your castle, Baron?" Princess Avery's smooth voice flowed from rosy lips that formed easily into the curve of a smile.

"Northwood is my keep, yes." An odd question. Though perhaps one stemming from her disappointment. While Northwood held a wealth of lands, he'd hardly consider the aged fortress of a kind with Leeds Castle to the south. What must a royal think of it?

"It's quite pretty. Not exactly how I imagined, though. Why do you have all that straw on the floor?"

Straw? "The rushes, Your Highness?"

"Oh, my. Is that a whole pig?" Her attention flitted to the servants bringing in the meal and laying it out on the center table.

"Does that please you?"

"What?" Her wide eyes slammed into him, capturing him once again. "Sorry. This is all quite new."

Worry wormed into his gut. A princess who had never sat at banquet? "If I may inquire, why has your father not joined us?"

Sadness replaced the wonder in her eyes, and regret took hold in his chest. Her shoulders rose and fell with a deep breath.

"He and my mother are both gone. I'm all that remains of my family, I'm afraid."

A daughter left without a male relative? Her kingdom had likely fallen into chaos. Had she escaped a rival seeking her father's throne?

He dared not ask directly, and so sought another approach. "I am not familiar with this kingdom."

Another emotion flitted across her face. It would seem the lady was incapable of keeping her thoughts contained. This time, something he would consider longing softened the corners of her eyes and tugged slightly on the corner of her mouth.

"No, I suppose you wouldn't be. Where I come from is very, very far from here. Oceans to cross."

Oceans? Had she come farther than across the channel? "How then, pray tell, did you know to arrive

this eve? And how long did it take you to travel here?"
Wilhelm had only been planning this feast since the turn
of autumn.

"Oh, I just kind of ended up here. Happens that
way, I guess."

She had an odd manner of speaking, one that set
him off kilter. Thankfully, a trencher arrived, allowing
him a moment to gather his thoughts. A displaced
princess without family had appeared in his barony
without escort. He eyed the woman, who'd told an
entirely unlikely tale. A woman dressed in such finery
wouldn't have survived traveling alone. Ordinarily, he
wouldn't think to speak in such a forthright manner to
royalty, but curiosity outweighed formality.

"Highness, if I may. How did you arrive safely
without escort?"

"I had an escort, I'm sure."

Had one? "They have stabled the horses and found
rest with my knights?"

"Uh…" She flashed him a smile that seemed unsure. "Nope. It's just me."

He was quickly losing confidence in her wits. She
hardly seemed a simple woman, with her intelligent eyes
soaking in everything around her and her expressive
mouth smiling at something across the hall she found
amusing. Yet her words made no sense.

She poked at the trencher. "Where are the forks?
And is this my…hmm." She fingered the slab of bread

holding the sliced pork. "My, uh, plate, or yours? Seems they only brought one."

"Here we share trenchers. Is this not so in your kingdom?" He waved a serving girl over to fill the princess's goblet. The poor girl nearly tripped over herself, wide eyes taking in the encrusting of jewels covering the crown atop the princess's head.

"No, this is not so." She twisted her mouth to the side in an amused fashion. "I've never shared a slab of bread topped with meat with a man I've just met."

His customs misaligned with her proprieties. He should not have assumed. He pushed the trencher toward her and snapped his fingers at a passing servant. "Another." The girl nodded and scurried away. "Do you not have a belt knife, Your Highness?"

"A what?" Her delicate eyebrows tucked together. "Why would I have a knife?"

"For meals." He gestured toward the meat in her trencher.

She craned a smooth neck to look at the other nobles filling the high table and then down at his knights and lower families below. "Huh. No, Baron. I'm afraid I don't usually bring a knife to a party."

He passed his to her without comment. He took to his own meal as soon as the pork and venison were placed before him—which included another knife given by a watchful servant—and kept his attention on the foreign princess from the corner of his eye. She poked at the meat, finally cutting a tiny slice and placing it delicately on her tongue. Then she immediately set the knife down and reached for her goblet. One tiny sip, and she pushed that aside as well.

"The food is not to your liking?" He hardly had the larders of a king, but he'd not thought the meal lacking. Especially as it had taken several hunting expeditions and the work of many hands to prepare.

She smiled sweetly, her royal manners obviously keeping her from speaking true. "I find myself too nervous to eat."

Nervous? Of course. He should have considered. Without her father here to make arrangements, she undoubtedly feared the manner of man she'd marry. And she'd certainly need to marry to find protection. But why so far from her home?

Sir Robert tapped a finger on the table, unable to control the thoughts running rampant. He had questions entirely improper to ask of a lady, especially a royal one. He raised his fingers, and a servant immediately appeared.

"Milord?"

"Fetch Wilhelm."

The servant scuttled off, and an instant later his steward stood by his side. Rising, Robert indicated the meal should continue, then bowed toward his guest.

"A moment, if you allow me, Your Highness. I must speak with my steward."

The princess tore her eyes away from the people in the hall, her interest in them as open as theirs toward her. "Yeah. Whatever you need."

He took that as her acquiescence and motioned Wilhelm toward the entrance to his solar at the rear of the hall. Once safely inside his private quarters, he pinned his most trusted man with a gaze.

"Who is that woman? She is strange, to be sure. And here to make a match? With a baron and not a prince? I do not know what to make of it."

Robert stalked around the room, his boots crunching rushes underfoot, while Wilhelm watched.

"'Tis a mystery, milord, to be sure. And to appear in her royal jewels." He shook his head. "Do you think them stolen?"

"If they are, I doubt they are so by her hand."

Wilhelm nodded. "What shall I do?"

"Send for Sarah. A woman will speak to another. Have my sister find out how the princess came to be on my lands and for what reason she seeks a marriage to a lowly baron."

His steward dipped into a bow. "It will be done."

He scurried out of the room, leaving Sir Robert with the strangely unnerving feeling that he was somehow being outwitted by a woman.

Three

*B*est dream ever. Avery smiled as women in the kinds of dresses she'd only seen at the renaissance fair and men wearing tunics and tights gathered in a grand hall that looked very much like something out of a story. Not the *Beauty and the Beast* kind of grand she might have expected of a fairy-tale castle. Instead of marble floors and gilded furniture like Belle had found, it turned out Avery's dream conjured a massive stone fortress featuring a soaring ceiling crossed with wooden timbers and gray stone walls lined with tapestries depicting battle scenes.

Fascinating. Why her mind had created this place as opposed to the castle in the opening of a Disney movie, she had no idea.

Well, unless of course it had something to do with the baron. He looked every bit the knight. And not the millennial-ized version on a Hallmark movie. Sir Robert was all rough edges and brawn with wide shoulders she would expect of a man who swung a sword or competed in a joust. A serious face gave him an aged appearance, though she doubted he'd had many more birthdays than she. And those eyes. Whew. No wonder her dream had brought her here. Who wouldn't want a medieval ball with a ruggedly handsome baron who looked at you so intently that you had a hard time keeping your knees from trembling?

"Your Highness? My lord has asked for me to invite you to join me at the hearth."

Avery turned from her bread-boat of a plate filled with rather unappetizing chunks of meat to look into the face of a young woman who shared the baron's rich brown hair and startling ice-blue eyes.

As soon as their gazes met, however, the girl dropped her gaze to the floor and dipped into a curtsy. "If it pleases you."

Why did she look so nervous? Avery guessed the girl to be around sixteen.

"Sure. I'm Avery." She held out her hand.

The girl looked at her outstretched fingers in horror and dipped lower in her curtsy. "I am at your service, Your Highness. Pray, forgive my forwardness. My lord brother wishes to know more about you, if you are willing to share."

Lord brother? Ah. The baron. He wanted to know more about her, did he? She sought his form in the crowd that had started milling around as the tables were cleared but couldn't find his among the faces casting glances at her.

Best play the part. She rose as regally as she could manage. "It shall be my pleasure to accompany you. May I ask your name?"

The girl's face reddened, and her eyes still wouldn't leave the floor. "Apologies, Your Highness. I am Sarah."

"Rise, Sarah. There is no need for you to keep looking at the floor. I'm not Medusa."

"Medusa, Your Highness?"

Avery shook her head. "Never mind. Come on. We'll go over here to the fire, and you can tell me what your brother wants to know. It's pretty cold in here anyway, and here I am in this frilly thing."

Sarah blinked, seeming dumbfounded, and then dipped into another curtsy before walking with steps that she obviously struggled to keep slow and even. They crossed the room, people parting out of their way with bows and curtsies. Avery had to do her best not to laugh. Laughing would totally ruin the princess fantasy. A princess would never do such a thing.

Avery smiled at the people as she passed, dipping her chin to each in turn. Finally, she and Sarah reached a massive fireplace at least eight feet wide. Inside, logs at least three feet in diameter produced blessed warmth, and Avery stretched out her fingers.

"All right. What does his lordship want to know?"

Sarah twisted her fingers together, keeping her eyes

locked on the floor.

"I'm not going to bite you." Avery tsked. "You can look at me. Let's talk. I'd like to know the baron's sister." Though she did wish the man would hurry up and return before she woke up.

Sarah's bright eyes snapped to her face. "Your Highness?"

"Just Avery is fine." Now that she felt warmer, she settled into a wooden chair a few feet away, motioning for Sarah to join her in another. Oddly, the people who had been hovering near the fire dispersed.

Sarah straightened, and her chin notched up a little. "If I may speak plainly?"

"Plain is good. No sense losing something in translation." Avery meant the remark in jest to lighten the mood, but poor Sarah only paled further.

"Yes, Your Highness. My lord wishes to know if you have come here as the other ladies have." Her gaze darted around the room, and she leaned closer and lowered her voice. "In order to seek a match."

A match? What was this, a Cinderella ball to find a wife? She nearly laughed. Of course it would be. Would she be the fairest of the ball, winning the handsome baron's affection in a sweep of romance?

"Sure. That's exactly why I'm here."

"But your father? Or another male relative to make arrangements on your behalf?"

Sadness stole the merriment of the moment. Why

couldn't the dream have included Dad? He could have been dressed in a silly king's costume and twirled her around as he had in her childhood memories.

"My father and mother are gone to God's embrace." Avery forced her voice to remain level. "I speak for myself."

Sarah's eyes widened. "For yourself?"

"Where I come from, a woman is able to speak for herself. Make her own choices on who she will marry and what she will do with her life."

"It must be grand to be royal." The words slipped out, and Sarah pressed her lips together, staring at Avery with a stricken expression.

Avery's fingers trailed over the jewels at her neck. "I'd give everything just to have my family back."

Compassion filled the timid girl's eyes. "Aye. I know what you mean. We lost my father, my mother, and two brothers. Sir Robert inherited Northwood and coffers that are—" She cut short. "I understand that pain, Your Highness."

Avery wanted to reach over and grab the girl's hand in a show of understanding, but she got the feeling Sarah might pass out if she did.

After a moment, Sarah said, "May I ask then, what has become of your kingdom without your father?"

The kingdom of Gardenia. A small house at the end of a country road where the flowerbeds overflowed with Mom's favorite white blooms. A place where she'd dreamed and imagined. An ache rose into her throat she had to swallow before she answered. "It's gone. I'm all that remains, and I'm afraid even I won't last much longer."

Avery shook off the thoughts. She shouldn't dwell on her diagnosis. She was supposed to be dancing and laughing, twirling around in a ridiculously wide ball gown in the arms of a prince—or at least a baron—who held her hand and fawned over her beauty. This dream was going the wrong way in a hurry.

"And your dowry, Your Highness?"

Dowry? Oh, right. The woman's gift to the man when they got married, since he would take care of her for the rest of her life. No shared bills there. She tugged her lip through her teeth until a thought occurred.

"Why, my royal jewels, of course. They will suffice?"

Sarah brightened. "I will let my lord know." She jumped up, and then as though remembering, dropped into a deep curtsy and stayed there. Not moving.

Avery stared at her a moment, then glanced around at the other people watching them. As soon as her gaze lit, people averted their attention. The girl still maintained the pose.

"Um, thanks. You can go now."

Sarah dipped her head lower and then rose and scuttled away. Well. That was weird.

How did a woman look both so regal and uncomfortable at the same time? From the shadows near his solar door, Robert kept watch over the two conversing women. The foreign princess seemed kind, treating Sarah gently and offering a ready smile. After a time, Sarah left the other woman's presence and gained his side.

"She is quite odd, brother." She fastened her hands together at her waist and gave him a pointed look. "Not that I've had any experience with royalty. She's not at all what I would have expected."

"She is foreign. Perhaps things are done differently in her kingdom than ours."

"As you say." Sarah appeared doubtful, despite her words. "She has no living relatives and said she would speak for herself as for who to marry. Have you ever heard of such?"

His eyes sought the lady again. She stood with her back straight, entirely unconcerned that her gown dipped to scandalous depths and her hair bore only the covering of her crown.

"She offers the royal jewels as dowry."

Robert snatched his gaze back to his sister. "She told you this?"

"Aye. Says her kingdom and family are gone. Her

jewels may well be all she has left."

Yet they would fund his barony for years. Give him the opportunity to right the wrongs of his brother and restore hope to his people. He could not have asked for a more advantageous match. Still, something nagged him.

"Why come here?"

"She says she is here to seek a match, and that she fears for her life. 'Tis my thought she escaped something terrible and is in need of protection."

A woman who arrived under the cover of twilight without escort would most certainly be in danger. Who or what had she escaped? Were the jewels even hers to give? What trouble would he invite were he to take her to wife?

"Thank you, sister. You have done me a service."

She dipped her chin. "The woman is odd but kind. She offered me her given name." Sarah gave a slow shake of her head, causing her veil to sway around her shoulders. "Perhaps she isn't royalty at all. But she is in possession of wealth that you need and seeks protection you can offer."

His sister had never quite mastered Mother's lessons on a lady's demure deference, being always too quick to speak her thoughts. An issue that would prove difficult when securing a match for her. At the moment, however, he found himself appreciating her directness.

"You are wise, sister."

She graced him with a knowing smile. "You shall protect us, even if it is trouble she brings. Father would approve the match."

Father wouldn't have wanted Robert to take the barony at all, nor would he have cared what match Robert chose, so long as the woman brought substantial wealth.

Another moment of consideration, and he stepped out of the shadows. What did a man say to a woman to work out the details of a marriage? Such things were done between men. Ladies let their gazes linger on him, and fathers turned their eyes away as Robert made his way across the room. Every man in attendance had known the lady Robert would choose the moment the foreign beauty had entered the room.

Lord help him, but her beauty did have a sway on his decision. Had she been less fetching, would he now be considering such a dangerous idea? He may well be bringing an army down on his head and a war to his king. Yet still he continued across the hall until he stopped a few paces from her. He bowed low.

"Your Highness."

She didn't curtsy. Perhaps she was royal after all. She merely tilted her head to the side and regarded him with eyes that spoke a language he couldn't decipher. "Baron. I'd started to wonder if you were going to leave me hanging."

Hanging? Her grasp of their language faltered. He

spoke quickly to spare her embarrassment. "I hope you'll forgive my lacking in such matters. I'm ignorant in the proper way to negotiate a marriage with a princess."

She looked at him for a long moment, something churning behind expressive eyes. "Where I come from, a man gets down on one knee, proclaims his undying love, and asks if the woman will marry him."

One knee? She wished him to kneel before her in front of all the nobility? A queen she was not. And certainly not his. Heat welled in his stomach. She kept his gaze, eyes smiling even though lips did not. Did she mock him?

"Here in Kent, a man negotiates with a lady's father, and the terms are agreed upon."

She turned out both palms. "You'll deal with me or no one at all. Of course, I'll settle for a dance, if that's what you prefer."

She toyed with him. His fingers flexed as a hush grew over the room. "Your jewels. This is what you offer in exchange for my protection as your husband?"

"You make it sound like a business deal. I'd like an oath of your love. Swoon-worthy romance and all that." She winked at him.

Winked.

Robert's chest tightened. How dare she make a mockery of him in his own hall? He took a step closer.

"I do not wish to be toyed with, Your Highness." He nearly bit off the title in an effort to keep his ire in check.

The jest in her expression faded, and she stared up at him with an unwavering gaze, refusing to bend under a look that had sent seasoned knights scurrying. Yes, definitely royalty.

"Then a dance is all you shall have. This is my dream, and we either do it my way or not at all. Besides, you were supposed to be a prince."

The words snaked out to bite him. Obviously, she was bitter over losing a suitable match. What had happened in her kingdom? But as she gazed upon him, all matter of defiance left her face. Vulnerability crept in, igniting a sense of protectiveness. A princess without kingdom or family. Forced to lower herself to a small English barony. Did he humble himself to her request?

A longing entered those warm eyes, dousing his pride. A life with this vixen would prove far more interesting than one with any of the other ladies present. Heaven save him, but in that moment he wanted nothing more than to give her the last bit of royalty she would find.

He dropped to one knee. "Princess of Gardenia. I offer unto you my protection and the place of lady of Northwood. You have my promise that I shall love you as a wife deserves, as our Lord God would require. Are we agreed?"

"Not exactly the proposal I'd hoped for. But then, none of this is what I'd *thought* I had in mind." She looked him over, forcing him to remain kneeling in her service. Suddenly, she grinned and dipped into a deep curtsy. "I bring to you all I possess in this world and pledge to be a goodly wife."

A laugh escaped her just as he returned to his feet. At least one of them found amusement in the situation. Humility, even to bring her such satisfaction, tasted bitter.

Princess Avery clasped her hands together. "This is the best game ever."

Game? His stomach soured, all thoughts of yielding to her whims vanishing. Marriage and the good of his people was anything but a game.

Four

The night kept getting weirder. Good thing this was only a dream. Otherwise, Avery might have been offended at the businesslike tone and the complete lack of romance in Sir Stern-Baron Northwood's proposal. She cast a quick glance at the stoic man standing beside her. He might as well have been one of the pillars holding up the ceiling. It was obvious he had not been pleased with her response.

She knew marriage wasn't a game. But none of this was real. Besides, the man had brokered a deal, not professed his heartfelt love and devotion. What did he expect from her?

This dream was going sideways in a hurry. Maybe if she concentrated hard enough, she could make some changes. Trade out the insensitive baron for a doting prince and the cold castle with floors covered in weird, reed-like plants for the grand ballroom from *Beauty and the Beast*. She'd keep the dress, though. Belle's yellow wasn't her color.

She stared at the scene before her, willing the view to morph into something regal, complete with her parents' smiling faces.

Nothing changed.

After the baron's awkward proposal, he'd called for the furniture to be cleared from the large hall. Once servants finished pushing tables and benches against the walls, three minstrels appeared from an archway and took a position near the baron's table at the head of the room. All three men wore the leggings and tunics in a style similar to the rest of the male attendees, though of a somewhat humbler appearance than those of the nobility.

It was getting difficult to remember this was all just a dream. Everything seemed real.

The air swirled with unfamiliar smells. Light danced from the roaring fireplace and from candles positioned on stands all around the room. Every detail filled Avery's senses. She'd known that her brain condition would hound her with neurological symptoms, but she hadn't expected such vivid dreams. Not that she was complaining. Interesting, lifelike dreams were a far cry better than the loss of memory, vision impairment, and lack of coordination the doctors had warned her to expect.

Even if she *had* ended up standing next to a stewing baron instead of on the arm of a handsome prince.

The merry sound of a flute suddenly livened the air,

followed by the rhythm of a hand drum harmonizing with a lute. Women in long-sleeved dresses and men in tunics gathered in several circles of six or eight and lightly joined hands. The people moved to the left in slow, graceful steps. Almost like a grown-up version of ring around the rosy. The dance looked simple enough. Avery cast aside thoughts of her impending neuro-degeneration and absorbed all the wonders of the medieval scene. She knew little about the time period, so she wasn't sure if what she saw was historically accurate or if her mind had simply pieced together tidbits from random movies.

"Are you enjoying the music, Your Highness?"

Sir Robert's deep voice startled her. Avery placed a hand to her jeweled throat. She'd been so caught up in her own thoughts that she'd nearly forgotten that the statue at her side knew how to speak.

Avery eyed the people moving around in a circle. "What is this dance?"

"'Tis the carole. You do not have this in your king-dom?" The baron kept a firm hand on the sword at his hip. The thing hung past his knee, giving him a dangerous feel.

"We have something similar, though it's usually for children. Adults dance as couples, not as a group."

"Your church approves of this?" His serious eyes studied her, their stark blue probing.

Avery thought a moment. That depended. When

she was a girl in youth group, some of the more conservative churches she had attended frowned on dancing altogether. Some sanctioned it as long as young couples left enough room between them for Jesus. She wasn't really sure about the church they'd started attending once Dad retired from the Air Force and they'd settled in Savannah.

"So long as it is tasteful, yes," Avery finally answered.

They stood in silence several more moments. Apparently, the man had no intention of asking her to dance.

"Now that we are betrothed, may I make inquiries?" His tone held a note of wariness she couldn't quite understand.

Under normal circumstances, Avery cleverly avoided personal questions. But since all of this existed within her own head, she could let loose a little. "Fire away. I'm an open book."

He frowned. "I do not understand this phrase."

Avery withheld a laugh. "I mean yes, baron. Please ask any questions you would like, and I shall answer them fully and truthfully."

His brows lifted. "I value your honesty, Your Highness. Thank you." He turned to face her more directly, his height about four inches taller than her five-three frame. "What happened to your father?"

A pain stabbed through her. Ouch. Right to the

worst question of all. Maybe her brain was trying to force therapy on her before she completely lost her ability to think clearly. Avery dragged her gaze away from those intense eyes, choosing to look anywhere else. "He and Mom were on their way home from the grocery store when a drunk driver ran a red light."

In one moment, she'd lost her family. Blake, her then-boyfriend, hadn't understood when she didn't rebound as quickly as he would have liked, and he'd ended things. Her only real friend took a job in Oregon soon after, and they drifted apart. In the years following, she'd dropped out of college and taken a job as an assistant party planner. She'd surrounded herself with surface-level friends, throwing everything into her job.

"Forgive me, Your Highness. I fear I do not understand."

Avery sighed. One would think her own dream would allow for the man to grasp modern concepts. "There was an accident in their...carriage. Neither of them survived."

He gave a stiff nod. "What happened to your kingdom?"

"There is no kingdom."

They watched the circles of dancers break apart and new people gather in squares of four for a different dance.

"I am sorry to hear of it. I vow that, as my wife, you will be under my protection."

It seemed he thought she meant that her kingdom had been lost. Not that her "kingdom" had been nothing more than a child's imaginings. She opened her mouth to correct him, but he spoke before she had the chance.

"As rivals will seek to dispense with the royal family members, I wish to know how to prepare." What was he talking about? When she didn't respond, his serious gaze bore into her. "My men will need to know if someone is coming for you."

Avery shook her head. "No one is coming for me. I'm entirely alone."

The hard lines around his mouth softened. "You are safe here."

His words slipped into a cold hollow of her heart, warming her in an unexpected way. She swallowed a sudden thickness in her throat and looked back at the dancers. "Thank you." She didn't know what else to say. None of this would last past dawn. Then, once again, she would be alone. The thought made her all the more eager to enjoy this moment.

Avery grabbed the baron's arm, determining to make the most of the bizarre situation her mind had conjured. "Dance with me?"

Surprise flicked across his dark eyebrows. "The dance has already begun. At the next, we shall."

"No, I mean just us." She turned fully to him and slipped her hands over thickly muscled shoulders. "We can dance right here."

Piercing blue eyes darkened from spring sky to stormy ocean, and Avery's heart fluttered. She looked up at him, too caught up in the intensity of his gaze to move.

"I do not know this dance." His voice came out low, washing across her like gentle thunder.

Pulse thrumming, she reached for his arm. He stiffened. Avery returned her hand to his shoulder. "You're supposed to put your hands on my waist."

He stared at her a moment longer, then lifted both hands and rested them at the curve of her waist, the warmth of them penetrating the layers of aquamarine fabric.

Avery cleared her throat. "There. Now, we simply move to the music." She swayed slightly, but he remained a pillar of stone. "Okaaay, maybe not." Maybe something more formal. "Here, how about this." She plucked one of his hands from her hip and held it out next to her in an old-fashioned waltz style. "You step forward while I step back. Then we make a square pattern with our feet."

That seemed to make more sense to him than swaying, and after a few moments, he took over the lead, moving them in a simple box pattern.

His mouth twitched, seeming to want to tic into a smile. "I like this dance."

Avery laughed. "I'm enjoying it too."

They made a few more squares before he spoke again. "I shall have the servants prepare a chamber for you in the family wing. Wilhelm will have your belongings brought up."

"No luggage. Just me and this fancy dress."

The baron's feet stopped. "You have no belongings?" His features sharpened again. "I do not wish to play games, Your Highness." He stepped out of her grasp, the spell of the moment vanishing. "You cannot have suddenly appeared without escort and without belongings. How did you get here?"

"I don't know." Avery huffed. "I woke up in your garden." At least, she kind of woke up. How exactly did a person dream waking up?

"This makes no sense."

Avery laced her fingers together. "One moment I laid down in bed, and the next I woke up here."

"You were abducted?" A shadow passed over his face.

She shook her head. "I'm here because I..."

The baron stepped close, his unnerving presence stealing the rest of her words. All the gentleness his face had held during their dance disappeared under the hard lines of a man who looked as unforgiving as drill sergeant. "I will defend against any who seek to invade this keep."

What? What in the world did that have to do with her waking up in the garden?

"Do not start games with me. I will not be seduced into neglect." Hard eyes slammed into her, and his nostrils flared. "Do you try to open the gates to invaders while I am distracted by your beauty and wiles?"

Avery's insides twisted, and she took a step back. What in the world was he talking about? They'd been discussing her waking up in the garden, and then suddenly he thought she was...what? Bringing an army to his castle? She would not let this dream morph into a nightmare.

In an attempt to regain control, Avery put her hands on her hips. "Seriously? I'm not planning some attack. No one is coming after me. My family is gone, and I will soon die." Tears blurred her vision, all hope of a dream's beautiful distraction now gone. "Believe what you will, baron. I don't care. I'm done here."

Before he could say anything else, Avery turned on her heel and strode for the door.

Robert clenched his hands. *Done?* What did she mean? That she no longer agreed to a marriage arrangement? Head held high, the princess stalked through the great hall toward two men-at-arms, who looked to Robert. He gave a nod, and they let her pass.

He'd posted more than enough guards to defend

Northwood Castle while they hosted guests, and his men were diligent. If brigands waited beyond the fields to attack, he would have the woman in hand as soon as the alarm sounded.

Though even as he assured himself of their safety, the thoughts felt foolish. If foreigners sought lands by such means, there were those far loftier than his.

Robert drummed a finger on his sword hilt. She'd seemed surprised by his accusation, then highly offended. Yet, something was amiss. Perhaps seeking the source had him grasping at unlikely notions.

Regardless, it would seem he had gravely offended royalty and had most likely given her cause to dismiss the marriage arrangement. What could he do to hold a princess to her word before vows were spoken?

His fingers clutched the comforting steel of his blade. He did not care to be faced with so many unknowns. Lack of information brought danger, and the strange woman who'd mysteriously arrived in his keep presented far too many unanswered questions.

He told himself he needed to seek other options if the princess had truly left as mysteriously as she'd arrived while he still had the opportunity, but his gaze would not leave the spot he'd last seen her.

Would she disappear into the night? She'd felt too solid in his arms to be a specter. And she'd been a bit too sharp of tongue to be an angel.

Wilhelm appeared at his side. "I have given her a

room by your sister, in the family wing."

How like Wilhelm. The man's ability to guess his master's wishes had served the Northwood family well. Robert grunted. "I wish to speak to Lord de Wirth."

"Milord? Are you not already in a marriage agreement with the foreign princess?"

"Perhaps." He stared at the archway, but the woman had not returned. "The princess may have chosen to leave us. I must discuss all possibilities while there is opportunity." His dignity would suffer the blow of a betrothal so soon broken, but he had not the luxury to nurse his pride. Northwood must have a dowry or the people would not survive the winter.

The steward hesitated for only a moment. "As you say, my lord." He bowed and hurried off.

Robert flexed his fingers, then, cursing his own foolishness, strode from the hall. No matter how she had come to him, he would not let a woman leave the castle grounds alone. Even if keeping her near would do naught but rouse trouble.

His men-at-arms directed him to where she had exited to the inner bailey. Outside, cold winter air tugged at him. She would freeze out in this weather without a proper cloak.

Remembering what she'd said about where she'd come from, he turned toward the rose garden, motioning two knights to follow.

"Come on, this is crazy!" Feminine frustration

punctured the night air.

He followed the princess's pitched voice down the path until he found her seated on a stone bench, her face turned up to the sky.

"Anytime now." She splayed her fingers, focus riveted on the stars.

"Your Highness?"

Her chin lowered, and she sought him in the darkness. He stepped forward slowly, so as not to alarm her. "To whom do you speak?" People who talked to themselves were suspect.

She rose. "God, I suppose. Or whoever is responsible for this mess." A strange laugh bubbled out of her. "Myself, maybe. Fat lot of good those doctors are."

This was how she prayed? And for what did she need a surgeon?

The princess pointed a finger at him. "I'm *not* lying. I woke up here. I should be at an inn with a weird lady in a sparkly sweater. I didn't plan to be here, okay? I just am."

She'd been at an inn? Had someone stolen her from her chamber and delivered her here? For what purpose? "You did not come seeking a betrothal?"

She barked a mirthless laugh. "Of course not. But when the opportunity presented itself, I thought, why not? But everything went haywire, so I'd just like to wake up now."

"Wake? You do not dream."

"Of course I do. None of this is real." Her breath came in spurts.

He should have her placed in one of the tower rooms for the night and then have his men escort her to the convent first thing in the morning. But something in the way her voice strained had him casting the notion aside. He had pledged this woman his protection. A hasty bit of foolishness or not, 'twas done.

Robert closed the distance between them and held out his hand. "I do not know what has happened to you, but I am quite real, as is your presence in my keep."

She stared at his hand for a moment, then slipped her fingers into his. He settled her hand on his arm and turned her back toward the castle. "We must get out of this cold before you catch your death of chill."

The princess allowed him to escort her back into the vestibule, then stopped.

"I'm really tired. Can I just rest now?"

"Wilhelm is having a chamber prepared."

"Thank you."

After a moment's hesitation, he turned from where his guests enjoyed the evening and guided her through the castle toward the family women's chambers. His thoughts churned, weighing every option.

"Are we still in agreement for the marriage?" He did not want to be the one to break his word, though he would gracefully release her if she no longer wished to be joined to him.

"I suppose." She kept her gaze ahead.

"And…your jewels as dowry?" Despite the woman's strangeness and the ills she may bring to his lands, the wealth glistening on her throat and catching the candlelight on her head were the salvation his people needed. Not even Wirth could come close to matching the like.

She sighed, then reached up and tugged the crown from her locks, leaving pieces of her flaxen hair sticking up at different angles. "Here. You can have it."

He accepted the proffered object, surprised by the gold's weight. "In England, it is proper to present the dowry at the wedding."

"How about you just hold on to it for me until then? It's starting to give me a headache anyway."

She trusted him with such wealth even before vows were spoken? With no knights or family men to uphold her honor, her faith in him stirred conviction in his chest.

"I will keep it safe for you, Your Highness. You have my word."

"No more of that highness stuff. I'm just Avery." Her shoulders drooped. She looked weary. More than that, forlorn.

Ah. He understood. Accepting his offer of marriage and turning over the symbol of her kingdom had stripped her of her rank. She would now be only a lady, the wife of a lowly English baron. His compassion for her swelled. As much as he'd lost in his life, she'd lost so much more. She'd lost her entire family. Her home. Her security.

He turned her toward the stairs and took a candlestick to guide their way to the upper floor.

"I pray you will find life here acceptable."

She didn't answer. They passed the door to his sister's room and found a chambermaid in the hall waiting to receive Northwood's new lady. He handed the princess off, and without a word she slipped away from him.

The door closed, leaving him with only the light of one candle to breach the darkness.

Robert fingered the jewels on the crown Avery of Gardenia had given him. She trusted him with her greatest asset. He would do nothing less than give to her all he had in return.

Decision made, Robert strode down the hall, his boots clomping on the wooden floors. No matter what unknown troubles she might bring, Robert wanted the fascinating woman as his own.

Five

Five more minutes. Avery sank deeper into the lumpy mattress at the seaside Victorian inn and pushed the vestiges of her dream from her thoughts. That had been weird. Her Creutzfeldt-Jakob disease, CJD for those who didn't speak medical nonsense, must be flaring up. Maybe she had less time than she'd thought.

Avery stretched and slowly opened her eyes, her surroundings coming into view as her senses began to function. She bolted upright.

No.

No, no, no.

This was *not* the room at the inn with the quirky Mrs. Easley. Nope. She couldn't possibly still be here in this strange place. Avery stared at the curtains wrapping around the antique bed, encasing her like she was in some kind of tent. Four big posts held up a wooden canopy over her head, allowing the heavy drapes to create green fabric walls.

This couldn't be a dream. Surely she wouldn't keep waking up while still dreaming...would she? With her brain condition, who really knew? Avery drew long breaths, willing her pounding pulse to slow.

Had she fallen into a coma and experienced a prolonged dream state? Comas weren't a part of CJD, were they?

Avery threw off a heavy fur blanket stitched together from who only knew what kind of animal skins and pulled back one of the curtains. She peeked out. Morning light filtered through the room's three narrow windows, struggling to dispel gray shadows. Everything looked the same as she remembered from last night. A large fireplace flanked by intricately carved wooden chairs stood opposite the bed. Melted candles dripped over the edges of a large round stand in the corner. A small eating table with two narrow chairs completed the furnishings. Everything was exactly as it had looked when she'd gone to sleep last night.

"I could use a little help here." The whispered prayer winged heavenward. Surely God would have mercy on her, considering her deteriorating peace of mind.

"Milady? Are you awake?" A chipper voice answered instead.

Avery withheld a groan. She'd forgotten about the girls. Last night, despite her protests, two teen girls who'd called themselves her "lady's maids" had insisted on sleeping on the floor. She was entirely unaccustomed to having other people in her room, and girls sleeping on her floor hadn't been a thing since ten-year-old sleepovers.

The curtains flew open, and one of the young maids smiled at her. The other girl didn't appear to still be in the room, and both pallets had been cleared from the floor. "Morning, milady. You must hurry. The lord wishes for you to join him in breaking your fast."

Avery shook her head. Oh no. No more grumpy baron. "I'd rather not."

The girl's brown eyes widened. "You must, lady. The lord has instructed."

Avery snorted. "Instructed? Who does he think he is to make such demands?"

"He...I do not understand, milady. Sir Robert is baron of Northwood. Your intended. He requires your presence."

Required, her foot. She didn't have time for stoic dream men. First, she needed to figure out how in the world to break out of here. Maybe if she had more information, she could force herself to think up a way to escape. Somehow.

"What's your name?" Avery studied the clean-faced girl watching her.

The slim girl dipped into a curtsy, her simple braid falling over one shoulder. "I am called Beatrice."

"And where is Northwood?"

"Milady?"

Avery scrambled out of the bed and stepped toward the hearth, where a fire flickered with life. "I know we're in England. But where, exactly."

"The Isle of Sheppey, milady." At Avery's confused look, the girl continued. "The region of Kent, south of the River Thames." She twisted her lips, and Avery wondered if the description had completed her geographical knowledge.

None of that helped Avery in the least. She'd heard of the Thames River, but she wouldn't pass any English geography tests. The fact that it sounded like a real place rather than a made-up one didn't help either.

"You know this not, Your Highness?"

Avery avoided the question. "No more highness stuff. I'm no princess."

Wide eyed, Beatrice nodded, but said nothing as she followed Avery on her trek around the room. "The lord will be pleased to have a lady such as you to take to wife, if you don't mind my saying so."

"I think he's more interested in my jewelry than me."

Beatrice didn't look the least bit ashamed for her employer. "Aye, lady. The dowry will be a great help to the people. We are all most grateful."

"Help how?" Avery paused by a window, but the glass barely let in any light. She couldn't see anything beyond it. Did all this dowry stuff go beyond padding a rich guy's pockets?

"Sir John, God rest him, left the coffers all but bare," Beatrice whispered. She glanced around, though no one else currently occupied the room. "The new baron sent for all the nobility to quickly secure a union and bring respite to his people. If not for him, most of the commoners would have starved already." Avery's expression must have registered her surprise, because Beatrice hurried on. "The wealth you bring to the lord's lands will keep us fed through the winter. Not many know how desperate the situation truly is."

"Then how do you?"

Beatrice shifted uncomfortably. "My father is Wilhelm, the lord's steward." She laced her fingers together. "I spoke out of place."

"No, thank you for telling me." The idea of marrying someone to take possessions of their wealth left a bad taste. But perhaps Sir Robert's actions could be redeemed if he did such a thing to try to help people.

Why any of it mattered in this dream world, she couldn't exactly say. Yet somehow it did. She had no idea where those jewels had come from. She hadn't even considered if they were real or costume. It hadn't mattered before. But now...

Avery rubbed the smooth fabric of her borrowed nightgown between her fingers. "Can I ask you an odd question?"

"Lady?"

"What year is it?"

Beatrice's face scrunched. "You do not know?"

"I'd like to hear you say it, if you don't mind."

"As you say, milady. 'Tis the year of our Lord, thirteen hundred and fifty-six."

Whoa… 1356? Why in the heavens would her brain conjure a castle in 1356? She didn't know what to do with that.

In a place she'd never heard of, for that matter.

The baron, his people, and their problems nagged at her. No dream should be like this.

There had to be a way out. Sleeping hadn't done it. Nor had returning to the garden. How was she to wake herself?

A knock sounded, followed immediately by the entrance of the other young woman who'd slept on a pallet on the floor. This one was taller and stouter than Beatrice's slight frame, her dark hair the opposite of Beatrice's blond. She carried something in her hand that she waved about.

"A letter for you, milady. I found it sitting right outside in the hall." She closed the heavy wooden door with her foot. "Perhaps the steward brought it but didn't wish to wake you."

"A letter?" Who would be sending a letter? Avery sighed. Why not? At this point, the sudden appearance of Queen Elizabeth, Pegasus, or a man wielding Excalibur wouldn't be any more absurd. She held out a hand and accepted the thick paper.

The tri-folded page looked to be made of thick parchment-type paper, with her name written in a fluid script on the front. Princess Avery. Weird. She turned the page over, finding the folded edge held a circle of red wax, stamped with a scrolling letter E. Avery slid her finger under the wax and released the seal.

Avery,

I fear you may be finding yourself a bit disoriented. Usually at this point I have a bit of advice for my guests to help them along with their particular journey. You, however, went to the tower room.

The tower room? She looked to the bottom of the letter, where it was signed simply "E." Mrs. Easley?

The tower room is for special guests, and you are one of a very few assigned there. While most guests spend a limited amount of time on their adventures, those assigned to the tower room are blessed with a more permanent transition.

Permanent transition? What in the world?

I'm sure this has come as a shock to you. It's my understanding that sometimes the Conductor chooses to send special guests to a new time and place if He wishes to give them a second opportunity. However limited your days may have been in your original time, the same will not apply to the new time and place He's assigned you to.

I hope this is of great comfort.

A great comfort? Was Mrs. Easley saying that Avery had been magically transported to a different time and place? And the Conductor? The way she'd capitalized the moniker and the pronouns pointed to... Did she mean God? No way. Was the eccentric Mrs. Easley really implying that staying in the tower room at her establishment meant that God Himself had transported Avery back in time to start her life over? Why not heal her, if that was what He wanted to do? She returned to the letter.

> *Whatever you may think, I assure you, your situation is very real. You are not dreaming. You are not in a coma. And you will not be returning to the place you left behind. He has offered you a fresh start, one without whatever physical condition you would have faced here.*
>
> *I pray many blessings on your new life, wherever the Conductor has taken you.*
>
> *E*

Avery stared at the letter. Read it twice more. This couldn't be real. Mrs. Easley seemed to be saying that Avery had been sent back in time. Permanently. Her gaze lingered on one line.

> *Whatever limited your days here, the same will not apply to the new time and place He's assigned you to.*

Did that mean she no longer had CJD, the terrifying disease that would rapidly break down her neurons until she could no longer think or function? And to do that, God, this Conductor, had sent her into the past?

That was crazy.

Avery returned her attention to the two girls pretending not to watch her as they made the bed. The floor under her toes felt real. The warmth of the fireplace and the hunger in her stomach felt real. Every moment since waking up in that garden—while fanciful—had felt real. Logical. Nothing that normally accompanied the flowing scenes of a dream.

But it couldn't be.

She held out the letter to Beatrice. "Put this somewhere safe for me, please."

"Yes, milady. I shall put it with your royal necklace."

The jewels. Had she been sent here with enough wealth to help save these people from starving? Why? If God wanted to rain down money, He certainly could.

Just like He could send you to the past if He wanted to?

Fine. Maybe she would follow this line of thinking, taking into account that God could do all things. Assuming that any of this crazy time-traveling nonsense made sense, of course. Avery pulled in a long breath. Okay. She'd been given the jewels to give to the baron to help his people. A mission of sorts. That was good. A plan to follow. She'd hand the necklace and earrings over as well, and then...

Oh no.

Her stomach bunched into a knot, and a wave of sickness soured her throat. She didn't actually believe the letter. But, what if...?

Avery waved a hand in front of her suddenly very hot face.

"Milady? Are you unwell?" Beatrice shared a look with the other serving girl.

Not good. Avery clawed at the fabric at her throat, her voice frantic. "Did I agree to get married?"

Beatrice smiled. "Yes, milady. We are all pleased to have you as the new Lady of Northwood."

Avery's knees weakened, and she dropped to the floor. Despite all logic, the truth pressed in on her spirit, bringing with it the choking realization of the stupidity of the game she'd played the night before.

She was actually stuck in the past. With no friends, no way to go home, and no idea how to survive. And surrounded by people who carried swords.

And she'd promised to be a stranger's wife. The room around her blurred, the edges of her vision fading into darkness. The floor beneath her tilted.

The last thing she remembered was Beatrice's surprised shout.

At least here he could find peace. Robert rose from where he'd knelt before the altar and hoped he could hold on to the feeling once he passed the chapel's doors. Today, he would take the visiting nobles on a hunt, then see them all off to return to their lands on the morrow. He suspected many of the neighboring nobility would have questions for him about his foreign visitor, though he had no answers.

He'd spent the majority of the night thinking and praying over what to do about the strange woman who had turned up at Northwood. Though he'd wrestled for hours, the only answer remained that which he'd already pledged to do.

Protect her.

He'd also alert his men and make preparations to secure the keep. No matter what else came of their relationship, the safety of Avery of Gardenia now fell to him.

He found Beatrice, a girl assigned to be the former princess's maid, waiting for him at the end of the hall.

"What news?" He barked the words, and the girl flinched. He needed to remember he was home from the battlefield, and lady's maids were not squires. He softened his tone. "Is Lady Avery ready to descend to the hall?"

"You must come, lord. She is unwell."

Words she'd flung at him last night surfaced. Hadn't she said she'd soon die? Robert quickened his steps, following Beatrice's dash toward the women's wing. He'd taken the princess to mean rivals would seek her death to cut off any claim to her throne, but perhaps she'd referred to an illness.

Beatrice burst through the door, leaving it open behind her for Robert to enter. Lady Avery, clad only in her sleeping gown, sat on the floor, one hand to her head.

"What's happened?"

She yelped at his words, hand flying to her mouth. She eyed him with the brazen look of one who was used to the fawning people did over royals. She held his gaze.

"Seems I fainted clean away."

"You what?"

"Lost consciousness. Passed out." She waved a hand around. "You know."

He knew what fainting meant. He'd not understood what cleaning had to do with it. "Are you unwell?"

She huffed. "I don't know. Maybe. Maybe not anymore."

Did the woman always speak in riddles, or was she merely seeking to vex him? "So you are well now?"

Avery rose, her maids steadying her. He couldn't help letting his gaze dip down from her face to the simple shift that didn't do much to mask her feminine attributes. She crossed her arms and glared at him. "I guess so."

He met her gaze. Were she not to soon be his wife,

he might have felt ashamed gazing upon a lady so. "I will wait in the hall while you ready to join me below stairs."

"And if I say no?"

Robert turned. She didn't want to accompany him? For what reason? "You said you are well."

"I'm fine."

The woman held his gaze as steady as any knight, fearless against a stern expression that had seen seasoned men back down. He drew a breath, trying to remind himself the lady felt out of place among strangers and grasped for any control she could find. He bowed. "If you are well, Lady Avery, then it would please me greatly to have my intended join me and my guests in the hall this morn."

She puckered her lips to one side. Making him wait. Finally, she bobbed a tiny nod.

"Oh, all right. But all I have to wear is that fancy dress from last night."

So that had been her hesitation. She'd not wished to embarrass him. The tightness in his chest loosened. "I have asked Sarah to find you a gown. There must be something among her and my mother's things that would be suitable."

"Okay." She twisted her fingers together. "Thanks."

He bowed again. "After breaking fast, I wish you to accompany me to post the banns before I leave with the hunting party."

Robert turned on his heel, leaving the former princess behind him muttering something about his manners.

Six

This was getting all too real. Avery stared at the two girls holding up dresses. Lora, the dark-haired one, displayed a deep green gown with little white flowers along the edges. "Lady Gwenllian's gowns will be too wide for you, but 'tis easier to draw in the waist than to add length to Lady Sarah's hems."

Avery withheld a sigh, channeling her growing fear into yet another prayer. If not for a healthy dose of that "passes all understanding" peace keeping a firm hold on her, she would have already freaked out. A castle. No way home. And engaged to a baron?

She nodded her assent to the wardrobe suggestion, and the two girls erupted into a flutter of activity. Time to get her facts settled and make a plan. She excelled at organizing details and dealing with the unexpected. At least, that had been the case when handling double-booked caterers and flooded party venues. She forced herself into work mode.

"What day is it?"

Beatrice glanced up from where she pinched fabric together at the waist of the green gown. "Wednesday, milady."

"And the month?"

The girls exchanged a glance. "December." Beatrice puckered her lips. "Three weeks until Christmas."

Avery submitted to Lora's tugging a white dress over the top of the one she was already wearing and then pulling strings, tucking fabric, and pulling strings again. "What about those banns the baron mentioned. What are they?"

"You do not have this in your kingdom?" Lora tugged again. "The baron must post at the door of the church his intention to wed. This is done so that if any have objections, they have the time to speak."

"And then?"

"Then you are free to speak vows, milady." She smiled brightly. "And just in time for the Christmas celebrations."

"Which will be better than we thought," Beatrice said. "Now that your ladyship has come to us."

The jewels, which had come from who-knew-where, would fund the celebration. Which would take place by Christmas...which was in only three weeks. The baron expected to wed her in *three weeks?* Avery shook off the panic rising up in her throat. No. No, she didn't have to actually go through with anything. At least he didn't demand to marry her tomorrow. A few weeks would give her a little time to figure out how to get home before she had to tell this guy she couldn't marry him. She had a bit of breathing room. He could keep the jewels, though. If she had them to give and they helped Beatrice's people, then maybe that was all she needed to do here.

Perhaps spending some time in the past would miraculously heal her CJD. Then she could return home. The lines from the letter poked at her thoughts, but she pointedly ignored the words Mrs. Easley had written. She *could* get home. There had to be a way.

She was certainly not spending the rest of her life in the dark ages. Even if the baron was slightly handsome and oddly intriguing.

Definitely not.

"Here, milady." Beatrice held up the dress she'd been working on and gestured for Avery to come try on the fabric.

This heavier dress fell in long folds over the layers of nightgown and first shift-like dress she already wore. The two girls tied a series of ribbons and strings that roughly adjusted the gown to her form, leaving little pieces of the second dress underneath visible.

"There. The length is good. I will be able to alter more of Lady Gwenllian's garments while you are out with Lord Northwood." Beatrice gave a satisfied nod.

"She won't mind?" Avery didn't want to pilfer some poor woman's wardrobe.

Lora shook her head. "The lord's mother passed into our Lord's embrace last winter, milady."

Her heart squeezed. Oh. These were his mother's clothes. Not knowing what to say, Avery gave a small nod of thanks.

"Sir Robert is the last of his line, milady." Lora's downcast features brightened. "Thus, you are a great blessing. Soon he will have the heir he needs, yes?"

Heir? Avery's stomach twisted, but she kept her thoughts to herself. No sense telling these girls she didn't plan on staying here long enough to wed a stranger, much less have children.

The girls shared a look.

"What?"

"We wondered, well"—Beatrice lowered her gaze—"'tis not my place, milady."

"What? You can ask."

Beatrice hesitated a moment longer, then shot out the question in a rush. "Have you married before?"

Avery barked a laugh. "Of course not." Why on earth had she worried about asking that?

Lora offered a sheepish smile that caused a dimple in her cheek. "Forgive us, milady. It's just that at your age…"

"My age? How old do you think I am?"

They shared another look, which seemed to be a regular form of communication for the two. "Never mind." Avery crossed her arms. "Don't answer that. I'm only twenty-four. It's not like I'm an ancient."

The girls dropped into a curtsy.

"Forgive us, milady." Lora spoke to the floor. "In England, ladies usually make a match many years sooner. We are ignorant of how things are done with royals. And with your kingdom's customs."

Oh, good heavens. "Stop all the bowing." Avery rubbed the bridge of her nose. Who would have ever thought that being unwed in her mid-twenties would have two teen girls thinking she was a dinosaur? She drew a deep breath and smoothed her features. She didn't want her frustration with the situation to sour any friendships she might gain. "It's not necessary. Really. I'm just Avery." She tempered the words with a faulty smile.

A knock sounded on the door, quickly followed by a gruff voice. "The guests are expecting my intended to join me at table."

Beatrice blanched, shooing Avery toward the door.

"I haven't even brushed my teeth." Not to mention that she needed deodorant. And a shower. Which she wouldn't get in a medieval castle. And her bladder may well burst before she dared to brave the dark, stinky room Beatrice had called a "garderobe."

Confusion covered the girl's face, but she blinked it away. "Quickly, milady." Beatrice thrust a rectangle of fabric and a metal wire loop at Avery. "Don your veil and circlet."

Avery took the two items but shook her head. The gown she could deal with. But she didn't need a wedding veil. The reminder hit a little too close to home.

The door suddenly swung open, and Robert swept a gaze over her, then gave a nod, his expression unreadable. "Let us go."

The man spoke like someone who expected everyone to jump at his command. Who did he think he was, some...yeah, okay. So he actually *was* the lord of a castle. That didn't mean she would bow and scrape and follow his orders.

Avery did her best to keep her composure, the extreme situation grating on every nerve. She held her head high and walked past the girls. She needed to eat, after all. And staying busy would keep her mind occupied.

Robert wore a long tunic that fell to his knees in a shade of green matching the color of her dress. Had Beatrice chosen this one on purpose? Both garments held bits of white trim, leaving her and Robert looking like a couple who had planned a matching costume for a Halloween party.

"The dress suits you." Robert offered his arm.

Feeling entirely out of place, Avery could only nod her thanks. She placed her fingers lightly on his thick forearm.

"I wonder why you do not wear the veil."

Avery shrugged. "I didn't want to."

To her surprise, Robert chuckled. "You are quite unlike any ladies in England."

He had no idea. They made their way down a long hallway, the interior wooden walls meeting the wide planks of the wooden floors. The castle's outer walls of stone had only small slats to let in the light, leaving candles to do the majority of the work even at this hour. Robert led her down a series of corridors, making turns she would never remember, until they came to a set of stairs. "I feel like I'm going to be lost a lot."

"Do not worry. You will soon become acquainted with your home." Her expression must have been dubious because he added, "I will have Wilhelm escort you around the grounds, if you wish, until you grow comfortable."

"Can't you show me around?" The words were out of her mouth before she could think better of them. She needed to spend less time with this guy, not more.

Robert lifted an eyebrow. "You wish me to show you the castle?"

"Well, yeah. I mean, it's yours, right?"

He chuckled again. "Your request pleases me. However, I am occupied on this day. Once the guests have gone, I will see if I can find the time."

She nodded, unsure why his words had that strange effect on her stomach. Probably just hunger. She hadn't eaten much of that deer-in-a-bread-bowl concoction they'd served last night. Hopefully breakfast would be better.

"Today we will post the banns." Robert led her down another hallway, the din of many conversations drifting toward them.

"No hurry. If you're busy, we can do that later."

Concern drew his dark brows closer. "We will post them today, as is proper, and while there are many witnesses."

The conviction in his voice stole any excuses she could come up with. Not that it mattered when they posted the notice. She wouldn't be marrying this man in three weeks. But that was a conversation they could have while he took her on a tour of the castle.

They entered the large hall where last night's ball had been held. Women wore gowns similar to hers, though all had the veils covering their hair. Avery hadn't even brushed hers. She reached up to touch the bundle of tangled curls she'd slept in. Yikes.

Oh well. Let them think what they wanted. Chin held high, she allowed Robert to guide her through the large space that reminded her of a cafeteria and to the raised table at the head of the room, where most of the seats were taken already. He pulled out a chair for her next to his in the center.

Once she settled, he sat next to her, immediately turning his attention to the man on his left. Avery drew a long breath, an array of smells assaulting her senses.

"A fair morning, Lady Avery. I trust you slept well?"

Avery turned to Robert's sister with a small smile. "Not terribly, I guess. Sleeping in new places is difficult, though."

Not to mention that spending the night six hundred years removed from one's own time could put any girl through an emotional wringer. Of course, she couldn't tell Sarah that, since Avery had been dropped into the middle of the superstitious age. Telling people she came from the future would be disastrous. They'd probably call her some kind of witch. And she doubted witches had comfortable rooms, lady's maids or any other privileges, much less the ability to wander around the castle looking for time-travel portals.

Sarah tilted her head in a very refined kind of way that somehow seemed out of place on a girl her age. "I have never been a night from Northwood. I can imagine it would be disconcerting. Especially without your own ladies in waiting."

Something about that last part seemed to hold a touch of both judgment and curiosity, but Avery let it slide. "You've never stayed the night anywhere else?"

"Once I was old enough, Lady Gwenllian became ill, and her care fell to me."

Lady Gwenllian. Sarah's mother.

Sarah nodded thoughtfully. "She would have been most surprised at my brother's choice, I think."

"Aren't we all?" Avery laughed. At Sarah's surprised

expression, Avery pressed her lips together. "I, for one, did not expect to find myself here."

Sarah lightly squeezed her arm. "Perhaps you have found this unexpected turn of fortune to be of God's design?"

The words hit a sore place within her, and tears welled. She blinked them away. "Maybe so. Still, it's a bit of a shock."

Sarah's soft smile warmed her face. "I will pray for you."

"Thanks." What else could she say? She needed all the prayers she could get.

Seven

rigands. The word knifed through Robert's gut, though he managed to keep his expression free of worry. "Where?"

"My man reported spotting them near Eastchurch. No farther than three leagues from you." Lord de Wirth swirled thin ale in his cup. "Seems they were wearing colors he didn't recognize."

Robert cast a glance at Lady Avery. Did she have something to do with them? Were these men who came from her kingdom? Despite her claims otherwise, he couldn't discount the possibility.

As though sensing his thought, Wirth grunted. "King Edward will not be pleased if foreign armies move on our lands." He popped a piece of cheese between his lips. "Especially not so soon after having returned from France."

"We do not know these men are foreign." Robert tore off a chunk of bread and rolled it between his fingers. "And if they are, we will see to them."

Wirth rubbed the thick whiskers on his chin. "You and I are not joined. Do not expect my banner men to rally to you, should these men move toward Northwood."

The jab landed hard, and Robert grunted. "You have my regrets that my arrangement with Lady Aldreda cannot come to pass. You know I must do what is best for Northwood and the people."

"A sizable dowry?"

One that made Wirth's considerable offer seem a pittance in comparison. "Enough to right not only what war cost us, but also to bring prosperity."

Wirth sighed. "I cannot fault you. I too saw the wealth the woman displayed." He drummed his fingers on the table, his voice low. "As I know you cannot fault me for not risking men in a fight not my own."

Robert ground his teeth but could not begrudge the man. "'Tis understood."

Beside him, Lady Avery spoke in low tones with his sister, their words too soft for him to make out. He still had a multitude of questions. Ones that would need answers before—

She bounced up from her chair, the sudden movement drawing everyone's attention.

In a scramble, men and women lurched to their feet, half-eaten meals on the table. Robert rose and gestured to the people that the meal had not reached its end. Benches scraped as the nobles regained their seats and conversations resumed.

"Well, that was weird." Lady Avery looked out over the gathered nobles and knights, her expression curious. Did subjects not rise in the presence of royalty in her kingdom?

Robert gestured back to her chair, his voice low. "I have not signaled the meal's end. You will regain your seat."

Lady Avery's eyebrows rose to her hairline. "What?"

"The meal. It is not ended." Why was she looking at him like that?

"Okay, that's fine. I need to go." She waved a hand at his chair. "But you can stay."

He could...? She thought to leave before he called an end to the meal, after he'd already had to fetch her to join him? And she expected *him* to obey *her* order that he stay while she left?

Not waiting for his response, the princess scooted out from behind her chair and strode down the steps of the dais, not caring that every set of eyes settled on her.

His men cast him questioning glances.

Growling, Robert followed and caught her by the elbow before she could scurry into the center of the room. He spoke low in her ear. "You are not royal here. I am baron, and you will do as I say."

Golden brown eyes flashed at him. "Excuse me?" She tugged her arm, and he released his grip.

"You should return to your seat." Why did this

woman behave as a lady should not?

Her hand settled on the curve of her hip. "Just who do you think you are? I can get up from the table if I need to." Her eyes narrowed. "What is this, a prison?"

Prison? She considered her place in his castle as that of a captive. "Of what do you speak?" He stepped closer, voice dropping dangerously low. "Are you not under my protection? Will you not be the lady of this keep?" He had risked a great deal to ensure her a place of comfort and safety. Perhaps at the risk of the brigands invading his villages.

She blinked at him. "What? It's an expression." She lowered her voice to a hiss. "I don't want to make a scene. I just really need to go to the bathroom."

Bath? She wanted to leave the hall in the middle of a meal to take a bath? He drew back, confusion unwinding some of the tension coiling within him. She took another step, and he caught her arm again.

"Don't." Her voice held an edge of danger he'd never heard a lady use. Almost as though he'd snagged a viper by the tail. Her voice notched up in octave. "Seriously. I've got to go."

If he released her now, all of his people would think him bested by a sharp-tongued woman. Nonetheless, her urgency tugged at him. "Why?"

"I told you, I have to go to the bathroom." The words almost seemed to pain her. Looking closer, clear discomfort tightened the corners of her mouth.

"What need have you of a bath during meal?"

"Bath? What? No, I—" She groaned. Those flashing eyes dug into him. She hissed words through clenched teeth. "The garderobe."

Realization slammed into him, and he released her arm. She must be sick indeed if she had need to leave the hall in such a fashion. Perhaps he should not have insisted she come.

She took a step back from him, her cheeks reddened in embarrassment. Sick or no, she still cast him a vexatious glare before stalking past him.

A troublesome vixen, to be sure. For some curious reason, the thought made him smile.

Really? Who did that man think he was? Avery didn't care if Sir Robert Control Freak ruled the entire kingdom. He couldn't tell her when she could go to the bathroom. Honestly.

Every eye in the room followed her. Some expressions held curiosity. Others, judgment. Sheesh. Who would have thought getting up from the table to go to the bathroom would be such an ordeal?

Heavy footsteps sounded behind her and soon the annoying baron gained her side. Oh no. He had to go with her to the bathroom too? What was with this guy?

"I don't need your help."

Sir Robert said nothing, his stride matching hers. She stalked through the straw stuff they kept scattered all over the stone floor, the heat in her chest pushing out the continual chill. Would the man follow her all the way to the toilet?

Not that there was a toilet. Nope. Just a cold stone bench with two holes opened to the frigid outside air. *Two.* Two holes. As in you could presumably find yourself sharing the facilities—and she used that word loosely—with someone else. Not to mention the lack of toilet paper. Or sinks. Or soap.

Avery stopped. Where was she? She'd gotten turned around in one hallway that led to another. They all looked the same. Where had Beatrice taken her last night? It had been upstairs, right? How had she missed the stairs?

"Perhaps I can be of assistance?" Robert's voice held a hint of amusement.

He found this funny? She wanted to refuse, but her bladder insisted that she swallow a little humble pie and accept his help. "If you'll point me in the right direction."

"I have a private chamber in the solar."

A private…like a master bathroom? The hope of finding something more desirable than what she'd visited previously pushed out her frustration at him sticking to her side. "Where's that?"

Stoic face showing nothing, he gestured her back in the direction they'd come.

"I don't have to walk back though all those people, do I?"

He lifted an eyebrow. "You do not wish to do so?"

Did not wish...? Of course she didn't. Hadn't the man embarrassed her enough already? "I'd rather not."

Robert gave a simple nod and turned down another corridor. Goodness, this place was big. Feeling a bit more like Belle and desperate to lighten the uncomfortable mood pressing down on them, Avery cleared her throat and forced lightness into her tone. "So, is there a library?"

"Library? This is not a monastery, Lady Avery."

Couldn't send me to a castle with a floor-to-ceiling library, huh? No dancing candlesticks and clocks either. Seemed like she'd only gotten the *beast* part in this *Beauty and the Beast* knockoff. She cut a glance at Robert. A lot less hairy, sure, but his mannerism could be just as gruff. And he'd even done the whole "You will join me for dinner" bit, right out of the cartoon. It had been breakfast, but still.

They came to a door, and Robert lifted a latch, gesturing her inside. Whoa. The room she'd slept in would fit in this one at least three times. A gigantic bed with drawn-back green curtains centered one wall, flanked by what she figured were two wardrobes. Across from the bedroom area, the massive space held a large dining table, a sitting area with several oversized chairs, and an office-type area complete with a desk covered in papers. Like a studio apartment, minus the kitchen. Thick rugs covered the floors, and tapestries hung from the walls. The biggest feature, however, was a set of wide, leaded windows. A pattern of geometric shapes glowed in the sunlight, creating a mural of color.

Avery walked over to them, running her fingers along the edges.

"My mother loved those. She said they reminded her of the abbey in London."

"Do they open?"

"In the warmer months, yes." Robert gained her side. "This pleases you?"

She looked up at him. "They are pretty."

Robert held her gaze, his face only inches from hers. He studied her, his eyes openly telling her he liked what he saw.

Her breath lodged in her throat.

Oh boy. She'd read one too many romance novels. Feeling breathless while locking eyes with a manly hero-type totally put the icing on this crazy cake. She told herself to move. Look away. Anything. Standing so close to a stranger who looked like he wanted to kiss her—even while her wayward brain wondered what that might feel like—was as sure a sign as any that she'd lost her mind.

He leaned closer, stark eyes holding her captive.

Would he try to kiss her? Would she let him? Her body took *that* moment to remind her of what had made her so uncomfortable she'd needed to leave breakfast in the first place. She stepped back, breaking the weird spell.

"Uh, the bathroom… uh, garderobe?"

"The door through there." He gestured across the room, his eyes never leaving her face.

Heat crawled up her neck, and she scrambled in the direction he indicated. *Oh, my soul and body. What in the world was that?* Avery fumbled with the latch on the door, finally got the thing to wrench open, and ducked inside.

The smell greeted her first, followed by the chill. The holes literally opened to the outside, almost like a giant porta-potty without the containment part. The waste fell right off the side of the castle into the water below. Though given the lack of plumbing, she supposed the design could have been worse. Nonetheless, she loathed it.

Scrunching her nose, Avery went through the process as quickly as possible. At least in the baron's bathroom there was a stack of small rags on a nearby table. A far cry better than the basket of moss she'd found in the other chamber. Something she'd refused to use. First thing on the to-do list: get Beatrice to make her a stack of toilet paper rags.

After getting herself as clean as she could and then using another of the rags to wipe her hands, Avery steeled herself to return outside. To-do item number two: tell Beatrice to put a bowl and pitcher of water in the bathroom for hand washing. Seriously. These people needed help.

Avery entered the chamber to find Robert still standing where she'd left him, waiting patiently. For some reason, the sight struck her. In her own time, two seconds of idle time meant pulling out a phone and checking emails or social media. She hadn't even missed her device. How weird. Of course, she'd been a bit overwhelmed.

"Shall we return to the hall?" Robert stood with his hands clasped behind his back, sharp eyes assessing.

And face all those people who clearly thought she was crazy? No thanks. "I think I'll go back to my room, if that's okay with you."

A crease formed between his dark brows. "I do not know this word."

"Which one?"

"Oak-ee?"

Avery snickered, and his frown deepened.

"Sorry. It's a word from my time, I guess." As soon as the sentence came out of her mouth, her fingers flew to her lips as though trying to smother what could no longer be contained.

Sir Robert stared at her. "You struggle with our language, Lady Avery. You mean that it is a word from your *place*. Time is the word we use to count the days and years."

Thank heavens he'd given her an out. Did she take it? Rather than correct him, she smiled. Keeping her mouth shut wasn't exactly lying. Right? The twisting feeling in her stomach said otherwise. But maybe that came from still not having eaten.

That had to be it. "Um, I guess I should eat after all."

His face remained passive, and he offered his arm. Avery placed her fingers in the crook of his elbow.

"Look, I'm sorry if I'm causing you embarrassment. All of this is overwhelming. Everything here is so far out of my league that I'm barely treading water."

The lines around his eyes creased once again. Right. Modern sayings.

"Let me rephrase. I find myself in a strange place filled with people and customs I don't know, and I feel very out of place." She huffed. "I'm nervous."

Robert opened the door to his private apartment space and then closed the heavy metal latch behind them. "I thank you for your directness. 'Tis not often I find a lady who speaks so. What can I do to help you?"

He wanted to help her? What she needed help with was finding a way home, but she couldn't tell him that. "I don't know." She laughed. "Get me a dog?"

That seemed to surprise him, but before she could tell him she was joking, a man with a sword on his hip and chain mail draping his chest jogged toward them with clanking steps.

"My lord?"

Robert strode from her side, reaching the man and bending his head to speak in low tones. As she neared, Robert swung around, his icy gaze pinning her.

His voice came out at a growl as he barked a command. "Take Lady Avery to her chamber." The face that had looked at her with such interest moments earlier hardened into beastly fierceness. "And see that she stays there until I return for her."

Before Avery could utter a protest, the knight had her by the elbow, and Robert took off down the hall.

Eight

"Aren't you going to tell me anything?" Avery pointed at the knight still standing guard outside her door. "It's been all day!"

The man, whom she placed somewhere in his mid-thirties, shook his head. "You know the lord's orders, milady."

Orders, her foot. The baron had commanded this medieval bodyguard to escort her to her room and see that she stayed. For no reason whatsoever. Beatrice had brought her both lunch and supper, and now the hallways teemed with night's shadows.

Avery stepped out into the hall. "And what exactly are you going to do if I decide to leave?"

The man stared at her, the expression on his hard face impassive. She may as well speak to a wall.

She took a step to the left. He mirrored and moved in front of her. She dodged to the right. He did the same. Feeling stupid, Avery crossed her arms. "If I run, you're going to grab me, aren't you?"

The knight nodded.

Avery groaned. "What's your name?"

"I am Sir Galahad."

Of course he was. Why wouldn't he sound like a character out of Robin Hood?

"Do you need me to escort you to the garderobe?" A hint of a smile tugged at one side of his lips. A jab at her earlier embarrassment? How did he know?

"No." She gave him her most pointed glare, but he didn't seem the least bit affected. Maybe a different tactic. She smothered her annoyance and forced a sweet smile and a honeyed tone. "Do you have a family, Sir Galahad?"

He gave her a wary look. "Aye."

"A wife? Daughters, maybe?"

"Two, milady."

Avery lifted one eyebrow. "How would you feel if some guy with a sword told them they couldn't leave their room?"

Sir Galahad looked genuinely confused. "If the action were for their protection, I would insist upon it."

Oh good gracious. The sugar fell from her tone. "When is Robert going to be back?"

"Lord Northwood will return as soon as he is able."

Avery didn't miss the emphasis on the title. Apparently not even his bride-to-be could call him by his first name. She rubbed her temples. "Okay, look. You are supposed to protect me, right?"

He nodded.

"So why can't you do that while I go somewhere else? Do you have any idea how boring it is to sit in a room all day with nothing to do?"

"I can fetch you some embroidery," Lora's cheerful voice came from the room behind her.

Sir Galahad actually smirked.

These people. Avery lifted her chin. "I'm going for a walk." She moved to step around the knight, but he once again blocked her path.

Avery feigned right, then shot left, but she wasn't quick enough. Sir Galahad never touched her, he simply refused to move out of her way. She considered charging him, but the man did look a little dangerous. Who knew what he might do if she pushed him too far?

She sighed. "Fine. Prisoner in a medieval castle. Just what I'd wished for. Stupid Mrs. Easley and her stupid inn."

"Of what do you speak, milady?" Beatrice poked her head out of the door, her expression concerned.

"Never mind." Avery cast one final glare at the man guarding her door and stepped back inside her room. "Maybe I'd have been better off with the CJD."

Robert patted the sweaty neck of Cesar, his destrier, and

swung himself back into the saddle. An entire day of riding, and they'd not seen the first sign of the brigands. Perhaps Lord de Wirth had been mistaken. A mixture of annoyance at not having put the matter to rest and relief that he'd not had to cross swords warred for control within him.

"Do we return to the castle, milord?" Sir Henry nudged his warhorse closer, the gray stallion a half hand shy of Robert's own black horse.

The two animals eyed one another, nostrils flaring. Robert put gentle pressure on the horse's side, and the creature relaxed.

Robert eyed the fading colors of a day spent. He had no desire to camp out of doors on a winter night. "Aye. We ride for Northwood."

Sir Henry tugged on the reins and trotted toward the rest of the ten knights Robert had gathered. Robert had wasted the time he'd meant to spend entertaining the visiting nobles, but such things couldn't be helped.

By the time they returned to the keep, the last rays of the cold winter sun had slipped from the sky, leaving the faint glow of stars to light their way into the castle. The men-at-arms on the outer bailey walls called for the gates to be opened, and his knights thundered through the portcullis with pounding hooves.

Robert handed his reins to a waiting stable boy and strode through the inner bailey and to the steps to the main entrance. A knight held the door for him, and he made straight for the hall. In his absence, Wilhelm had seen to the guests' needs.

To his relief, Lady Avery did not preside over his hall in his absence, only Sarah lingering at the table. He made his way past the lower tables and to the dais with minimum stops to greet the visiting nobles, then finally gained his chair.

"I have news, brother." Sarah leaned toward him as soon as he'd gained his seat. "I fear you will not like it."

Robert clenched his teeth and gestured for a serving girl to bring his meal. "Lady Avery?"

Sarah nodded. "She put up quite a fuss at your containment, brother. It leads me to wonder why."

"Did you ask her?"

Sarah drew back.

He didn't mean to bite off the words. He blew out a breath and softened his tone. "Did she give reason to be mistrusted?"

"I did not seek her company. I learned this from Agnes."

Sarah's maid. She'd been with Sarah since she was a girl, and Sarah loved the woman like a mother. His sister's affection for Agnes remained the only reason Robert tolerated her. Never in his years had he seen a woman more intent on inserting herself where she didn't belong.

"Agnes spoke to her, then?"

Sarah lightly lifted her shoulder. "She spoke to

Lora. 'Tis the same."

The serving girl returned with a trencher of stewed venison, and he set to the meal with vigor. "We must remember that Lady Avery is used to being royalty. I suspect she will chafe at following orders."

"And if she brings trouble?" Sarah lifted an eyebrow.

"Then I shall handle it. Such is not for a lady to worry over."

Sarah turned her attention back to the room. She tapped one delicate finger on the table, considering. Robert finished three bites before she spoke once more. "There is another matter I wish to discuss."

Her own marital arrangements. Something he was supposed to have seen to this day. "Since we did not go on the hunt, I have not had the time to discuss possible arrangements with any of the nobles." He dared a glance at his sister's pinched face. "Fear not, sister. With what the foreign princess brings, I will be able to replace what William lost. You will not be without dowry. We will have options."

She gave a hesitant nod. "My concern lies elsewhere." She ran a finger over the edge of her goblet, more pensive than he remembered seeing her.

"Speak, sister." Robert poked another bite, his hunger from riding all day gnawing his insides. Sarah need not fear he would not find a good match for her. With the wealth Avery brought, he could afford to find her an honorable husband and a place as noblewoman.

"I wish to choose my own match."

The declaration stilled his hand. He followed her gaze to the lower tables. Someone here? Odd. Most of the men visiting were fathers of the ladies brought to Northwood for Robert. "Who?"

"Sir Henry."

The name slammed into him, and he nearly dropped his knife. His sister held affections for his most trusted man-at-arms? How had he not seen this?

"Before you say anything about him being landless, I do not care." Sarah lifted her chin in the defiant way that had always annoyed Mother. "It is my wish to stay here anyway." Her eyes softened. "At my home. With you."

Robert opened his mouth to protest, but she leaned closer, her voice soft. "I do not need to be the lady of a castle. I wish only to lead a simple life with the love of a husband and children of my own to rear." She looked at him with such longing that his stomach twisted.

He'd pictured his sister going to a landed lord. Someone who would strengthen their ties to another noble. "A noble will be better able to care for you, sister."

"Where you, with the crown jewels of a foreign kingdom, cannot?"

Robert gripped his knife, pressing the handle into his palm. "You do not wish for more?"

"What is more important than love?"

Robert sought out his knight, finding the man watching him with a tight expression. Did Sir Henry guess their conversation? "And Sir Henry?" He kept his eyes on the knight, pleased the man did not look away as though ashamed. "You think he will give you what you desire?"

"Yes." The word held tenderness, hope.

Something within him pricked like a thorn. He'd entered into a marriage arrangement in order to care for his people. His sister only wanted what her heart longed for. Had Lady Avery held hopes for a love of her own? Did she settle for him? Would a woman ever speak of him with such yearning as his sister spoke of Sir Henry?

Would Avery?

Pushing the thought aside for consideration later, he focused on Sarah. "Does Sir Henry share your affections?" His eyes bore into hers, searching for any sign that the man had taken liberties. His best knight or not, Robert would have the man flogged.

Pink tinged her cheeks. "I hope he does. His honor binds him, and he thinks the same as you. He is a landless knight and would never seek his lord's sister's attentions." She sighed. "Yet still he has found them."

Robert narrowed his eyes at the knight, and Sir Henry shifted. He held the man's gaze a moment, then returned his focus to his food.

Robert jabbed a chunk of venison. "I will consider

the matter."

"I thank you, brother. 'Tis all I ask."

He raised his knife once more, the matter settled.

"Now let us discuss you." Sarah's eyebrow arched.

The venison paused again on its way to his mouth. "There is naught to discuss. 'Tis done. I will wed Lady Avery in two weeks' time."

"Two? I thought it three, right before Christmas."

"I see no need to wait. I would do it today, were it not for the priest's insistence." The sooner he had the matter settled, the better. If brigands lurked in Northwood seeking their lost princess, he'd sooner they found her already his wife. But he would not defy the church.

"Do you think you could grow to care for her?" Sarah searched his face with an odd intensity. Why did she question him so?

"She intrigues me." The honesty of the answer slipped out as easily as the words. He chewed a bite thoughtfully and swallowed. "I believe it is possible for affection to bloom once we are wed."

Sarah slid her hand over his forearm. "I wish for your happiness, brother. Not only the security of Northwood."

Affection for his sister filled him, and he offered a smile. "Then pray God will make it so."

A light glinted in her eyes. "That prayer, dear brother, I have already spoken."

Avery was going to skin that man alive. She paced around the room, fuming. If he had any notion that she would even *think* of marrying him now...

"Milady? Would you like for me to fetch something from the hall for you?"

Avery spun on Lora. "Yes. Mr. Baron Thinks-He's-All-That."

"Milady?" Lora twisted her fingers together, clearly confused.

"Really." Avery threw up her hands. "Who does that man think he is? Locking me in my room like I'm a prisoner." She pointed at the door where the stoic knight still stood guard on the other side. "He's back. Did you know that? Back and having his meal in the hall while keeping me locked up here like...like...some pet. No. Not even that. Dogs have it better."

Lora's eyes widened with each line of Avery's tirade until they looked like they would pop right out of her head. "The lord isn't keeping you captive, lady. He fears brigands seek to capture you and wishes for your protection."

The girl had told her this three times already. As had Beatrice. And Sir Galahad. Repeating the placating words again did nothing to ease her frustration.

"He does this out of affection, lady." Beatrice

stepped closer, voice soft and entreating.

Avery deflated. Maybe the barbaric man really did think he was keeping her safe. That didn't excuse him locking her away, though. "I hate sitting around with nothing to do. I like keeping busy. Being around people." She gave a little shrug. "At least I didn't get locked in here alone." She included Beatrice in her glance. "Thank you both for keeping me company and trying to help me stay occupied."

Small smiles flitted on their lips, but both remained silent.

Avery huffed and dropped down on the bed. "Would you like to know what I do back home?"

"What is that, milady?" Beatrice sounded genuinely excited. "I would love to know what duties a princess performs."

"Not that." Avery shook her head. "I mean my job, not that…title."

Beatrice and Lora shared one of their looks.

"I mean how I spend my days. I plan parties. Events. Make sure that everyone knows where they are supposed to be. Design the menus, direct the caterers. I create special celebrations for people's most important nights." Avery sighed. She really had loved that job. She'd always felt a sense of accomplishment, seeing the perfect night come together.

Lora beamed. "Aye, lady. Like you will do here, once you wed the baron."

"What?"

"'Twas what Lady Gwenllian did." Beatrice nodded gleefully. "She directed the servants, planned the menus for the cook, and organized visits for the nobles. You will not be without this work here."

"Yes, milady," Lora added. "It is the same. Perhaps our kingdoms are not so different."

Huh. She'd never thought about what a lady of a castle might do. Could her skills at directing crews of people really come into play here? Having a purpose and interacting with the population of the castle—that was exactly what she needed to keep from losing her mind in sheer boredom.

Assuming she truly was stuck here.

That little voice inside pressed on her again, insisting her situation would be permanent. If that was true, then maybe running the events of the castle wouldn't be so awful.

Except for the fact that the job came with that...that...caveman. Ugh.

A knock pounded on the door. Beatrice scurried up from her place near the hearth and cracked it open.

The baron's loud voice pushed past her. "I will see Lady Avery now."

"Oh, you'll see me all right." Avery snatched up her skirts and marched to the door. "Girls, you might want to enjoy a little time to yourselves." Avery flung open the door and shooed the two nervous maids out into the hallway.

Time for Baron Northwood to learn exactly who he was dealing with.

Nine

The woman resembled a hornet. Small and buzzing with fury. Robert held his hands behind him, patiently waiting out her tirade over having been confined to her chamber.

"….and, and well." Lady Avery huffed and threw up her hands. "Do you see what I mean?"

He considered her. She huffed, settling her hands on her hips in a posture of defiance. She'd spouted a lot of things, primarily that he did not have the right to keep her under guard. He gave no response to that. As Lord of Northwood, he had every right. Therefore, that argument held no merit. For what, then, did she boil with venom? "Did keeping you here thwart plans to conspire with the brigands?"

"Conspire with the…? Are you out of your mind?" Avery glared at him, her eyes flashing ire. "Is that really what you think? That I came here with some plan to bring bad guys down on you?"

Robert tested the meaning of her strange wording,

deciding she meant bringing the brigands to his land. "I am not sure what to think. Only that you appeared at the same time as they."

She rolled her eyes toward the ceiling. "No. I did not bring any *brigands*. Or anyone else for that matter. No one is coming for me. No one that I know, or that is in any way connected to me, is coming to attack you. I'm not conspiring with a single person on this planet. Are you satisfied?"

"So you say." Robert spread his palms. "Yet I cannot help but think you hide something from me."

Avery groaned. She closed her eyes, drawing a long breath. After a moment, her eyes shot open. "Fine. You want to know the real truth?"

"I always welcome truth." He prepared himself to receive confirmation of his suspicion that she knew a fight would be coming to Northwood. Did she still not believe he would protect her even when she admitted to knowing trouble would come?

"I'm from the future. I have a brain disease. I was supposed to die, but Mrs. Easley said that God sent me here instead. Some kind of second chance." She crossed her arms, expression wary.

Robert tried to process the jumble of words. Future? As in a time yet to be? Likely the lady meant something else. "A brain disease?" That would explain her distemper. The church would grant a dissolution of his intentions if his bride suffered from a lack of wits.

Strangely, the idea brought a sadness he couldn't comprehend. Lady Avery didn't appear to lack wits. An odd woman, most assuredly, but not one wanting for intelligence. Perhaps unfamiliarity with his language caused confusion. He returned to the other part of her declaration.

"This word you used. *Future.* I do not think it means what you think it means."

She burst out in laughter.

Robert drew back in confusion. Perhaps she *was* mad after all. He frowned, unsure how to respond to the outburst.

"You just quoted *The Princess Bride*, Inigo Montoya." Avery leaned forward, wiping moisture from her eyes. "That's priceless."

Robert struggled with her meaning. "A princess bride? This is you, yes?" The woman laughed again, and Robert deepened his voice, commanding her attention. "Who is this Inigo Montoya?"

She waved a hand. "Never mind. I can't even start explaining movies to you." She sobered and took a deep breath. "I know what the word 'future' means, Baron. It means a time ahead of this one."

If she hadn't misspoken, then perhaps lacking wits would be the least of his worries over Lady Avery.

"You're in the fourteenth century. I'm from the twenty-first." She pointed a finger at him. "And before you say something stupid, no, I am *not* any kind of witch. I cannot be, of course, because I am saved and sealed by God." Conviction filled her voice, and her eyes dared him to dispute her.

Robert ground his teeth, unsure what to do with the woman's wild claims.

"It's a lot to take in. I get it." Avery's expression softened. "This is the best I can do to explain. I went to a doctor, and he told me I had an incurable condition that would make me start to lose my memory, then my muscle functions. Eventually, my internal organs wouldn't work anymore, and I would die. Before that could happen, I decided to take one last trip to see and do as much as I could.

"One of those places happened to be an inn. I saw a family tree hanging on the wall and…" She trailed off. "Huh." She shook her head, looking confused. "I saw my name listed next to yours." Her eyes searched his as if he would be able to make sense of what she was saying.

"Anyway," she continued, "I went to bed, and I woke up in your garden, dressed like a princess. I thought I was dreaming, so I went with it."

The story made less sense the longer the woman talked. Robert held up a hand. "Is this why you said you were dreaming in the garden and were praying at the sky?"

"Yes. I wanted to wake up. Go home."

"You arrived in my garden with no memory of how

you came to be there, then told my steward you were a foreign princess."

She twisted her hands in front of her, worry creeping onto her expression. "Yeah."

"Are you a princess?"

Avery straightened her shoulders. "My father always said I was. But, no. Not in the sense you think."

Alarm washed through him. "The jewels? Did you steal them?"

"No." Her response shot forth with conviction. "I got them the same way as I got the dress."

Robert rubbed his temple, the absurdity of this conversation grating on him. "You speak without sense, Lady Avery."

"I'm sorry." Tears filled her voice. She turned away from him and settled in one of the hearth chairs. She lowered her head. "I didn't ask to be here. I didn't purposely come here dressed like a princess with all those jewels. I didn't mean to accept your proposal because I thought all of this was a dream."

The sadness and vulnerability in her voice clutched him in a way he couldn't explain. Before he thought better of the move, Robert closed the distance between them. He dropped to his knee and cupped his hand under her chin.

She looked up at him with shimmering eyes, the emotion in their depths igniting a fierce desire to comfort and shield her. He knew he could not afford to be enchanted by a woman's wiles. Though, even as he reminded himself that danger stalked such a path, he felt himself slipping closer in that direction. Lady Avery did not appear to be using feminine charms against him. She seemed genuinely distraught.

"I really am sorry, Robert," she whispered. "I didn't mean to lie to you."

He rubbed his thumb across her cheek, wanting to believe her.

"I'm from the United States of America. Hundreds of years from now, your country will lay claim to a land across the ocean. You will make colonies there. Many years later, those people will revolt and form their own nation. That nation is where I come from." Her eyes pleaded with him to understand something he could not.

How could she expect him to believe such? Yet, as ridiculous as the claim sounded, he found himself wanting to trust her. Though what she spoke made no sense, it was clear she believed her words with deepest conviction. The urge to accept the impossible tugged him ever closer, like a moth winging too close to the flame.

"You did not mean to accept my proposal of marriage?" Of all the things he could have asked, perhaps should have first inquired after, his heart instead spoke the one question that mattered most.

The corners of her eyes tightened. "I thought I was

dreaming. A handsome baron, lord of a castle, got down on his knee and offered a life together. In my heart, I wanted to accept your proposal, even though I didn't think any of it was real."

Her softly spoken words latched onto him. He needed to get to the chapel. Pray over what to do with the unnerving creature who had upended his life. At the moment, though, all he could feel was an overwhelming desire to protect her. Shield her from the dismay claiming her beautiful features.

His fingers caressed her smooth cheek. "Do you wish to marry me, now that you know I am real?" An absurd question, but one he must ask.

She sucked in a sharp breath, eyes widening. "Would you want to marry me if I didn't come with a sack load of wealth?"

The question stung in a way it should not. Marriages were often arranged for such benefits. Love and affection came after. He thought of his parents, who'd despised one another and could barely speak whenever they were forced to share the same space. With Avery, he'd felt enough stirring within him to hope they could at least develop an amenable companionship should they wed.

He considered her question, giving it due thought. Finally, he nodded. "I would want to, yes. Yet what I want matters little, I'm afraid. Without your dowry, I would have made arrangements with Lord de Wirth to wed his daughter and join my lands with his."

Disappointment lowered her eyes, and he placed a finger under her chin, asking her to look up. "Lady Avery. I must first see to the needs of my people. I cannot ask them to starve so that I may indulge myself, no matter how fascinating the woman I wish to wed."

"I understand." Her voice held sadness. "After my diagnosis, I never expected to wed at all." She straightened, the traces of vulnerability in her features disappearing. "I would like to offer you the crown and jewelry I brought here. They are yours. Use them to care for your people without the obligation of marrying me."

Robert's chest stirred as his heartbeat quickened. "You mean this? You would give up all the security you have for my people? Why?"

Avery shrugged. "Like I said. I was sent here with it. It must have been so that your people could survive. I won't deny Beatrice, Lora, and anyone else here the help I can give. Those jewels were given to me, and now I give them to you."

The solution to his problem stared him in the face. She offered the wealth freely. He could allow her to live here as a ward or send her to the safety of the convent and still feed his people. He did not have to enter a union with a woman who admitted she would soon be without her faculties. The symptoms of her disease were obviously already emerging, since she did not know how she came to him and thought herself from a kingdom that was yet to be.

"I must pray over this." The stirring in his heart to take Avery in his arms and make her his own put a pressure on him he could not escape without prayer.

She nodded. "I'll do the same." She sighed. "I know how the story sounds. I know it doesn't make sense. But I believe I'm going to have to spend my life stuck in this century." Again, moisture filled her eyes. "Why I was sent to you, I don't know." A small laugh bubbled out of her. "Medieval times wouldn't have been my first choice. But that isn't your burden to bear."

"You are always welcome at Northwood." Robert stepped close to her, meaning the words. The woman called to him in ways he could not comprehend. Could he truly allow her to live under his roof and not take her to wife? He clenched his teeth. He must pray.

Avery's eyes questioned him, stirred him.

He should not take liberties until he decided if he would take her to wife. Should not. Yet, as if of its own accord, his hand reached for her. His fingers cupped the back of her neck, nestling in the softness of her flaxen hair.

"Robert, I…" She whispered his Christian name with echoes of the longing that churned within him.

Gently, he lowered his mouth to hers. The sweetness of her lips melted into his own, and passion burned hot within him. He drew her closer, drinking in her softness.

She moved into him, her arms clasping around his neck.

He yanked his head back. "We should not." He did not trust himself to keep control of the desire flaming to life within him. "I must first pray."

Avery stepped out of his arms, nodding.

He would pray. But Lord help him. He already knew what *he* wanted.

Ten

*N*ow what was she supposed to do? Avery's pulse fluttered like a hummingbird trapped in a cage. She'd prayed, considered, and prayed some more. The answer pressing on her heart remained unmovable.

She wouldn't be going home.

Not that she had much to go back to. In her own time, she would live less than a year, her brain casting off bits of her memory like a bath bomb dissolving in water until nothing remained. That fact didn't negate the worry quivering through her. Living life outside of one's own time brought very real fears, even if she had been healed from her CJD. What this era lacked in modern conveniences it made up for in difficulties. And not simply because they lacked basic sanitation.

Why would God send her here? She'd gladly take the healing. Maybe even be on board with a life in the past. But here? Early nineteen hundreds she could have lived with. They had electricity. Decent bathrooms.

This place was…barbaric.

Beatrice tugged a comb through her hair, trying to work through the knots Avery's night of tossing and turning had produced. She'd risen early, washed as best as she could with lukewarm water and a rag, and scrubbed a cloth against her teeth in an effort to gain at least a measure of cleanliness. Apparently these people chewed on a twig until it frayed and then used that to scrub at their teeth. No thanks.

Today she would see the baron again. After his declaration two nights before that he needed to pray, he'd spent the entire next day out on a winter hunt with the visiting nobility. Her maids had asked if she wanted to spend the day in the hall with the other women, but she'd declined, opting to stay in her room.

The irony wasn't lost on her. But she'd needed the time. They didn't have any Bibles, but Beatrice had brought her a copy of Lady Gwenllian's psalter, a small book with the Psalms. But the entire thing was written in Latin. Still, Avery enjoyed looking at the beautiful artwork as her heart recalled verses of God's protection that she'd long ago memorized.

"I am pleased you are feeling better today, milady." Beatrice tugged on a particularly difficult knot, snatching Avery's head backward.

She withheld a groan. "I think my situation was more to blame than any illness. Too many new things and no chance of going home."

Beatrice patted her shoulder. "I've been praying you

will be happy here." Another few tugs. "And that you and the lord will find joy in your arrangement."

"You've been praying that?"

"Aye, milady." She pulled up a lock of hair and twisted it toward the back of Avery's head. "And Agnes says that Lady Sarah has gone to chapel every morn, praying for a love to grow between you and her brother."

People had been praying for some kind of spark to happen between her and Robert? Could that be why she felt this unexplainable draw to a man she barely knew? She pushed the thought aside. It didn't matter. At least, not now. There was no way she was going to marry someone—anyone—in a matter of weeks.

Maybe if she stayed here and they got to know one another over a reasonable amount of time—a year or so—she'd consider it. Now that he had the money he needed for his people, he wouldn't feel like they had to rush things. They could take their time. She planned to discuss that option with him today.

If she really was staying, then she had to acknowledge the other answer she'd been given during her long hours of prayer. Something was happening in her heart in regards to Baron Northwood, and God hadn't given the first warning to steer clear of the man. In fact, every time she thought of a life with him, peace settled over her.

Who would have thought getting a sense of peace

could be so troubling?

Beatrice placed a length of thin cloth over Avery's head and secured it with a circlet that fit over her forehead. She'd once again put on two dresses, the one underneath a pale green. The top dress, a very light pink, had slits along the arms to show the highlights of the green one.

Hair finished, Avery stood. "Well, how do I look?" She rubbed her hands down the front of the fabric, lines of embroidery sliding beneath her fingers.

"Beautiful, milady." Beatrice grinned. "Milord will be most pleased."

Strangely, Avery hoped he would. Time to get this show on the road. "Guess this is as good as it's going to get. Let's go eat."

Beatrice led her through the long hallways and down to the first floor. Avery paused at the entry to the great hall, stomach fluttering. The room teemed with people laughing and talking where they gathered around the lower tables. Scents of people, meat, and warm bread hovered on the still chilly air.

She grabbed Beatrice by the arm. "I thought you said we were up early."

Beatrice leaned close, matching Avery's whisper. "We are, milady. What is amiss?"

"Nothing." Avery sighed and released the girl, granting her the permission she sought to find her own meal.

Avery had hoped to beat the baron—and most of his guests—to the hall. Arriving first would have given her a sense of control that walking into a crowded room did not. Nothing for it now. He'd already spotted her.

Robert rose from his chair and gestured for her to enter. No one else had joined him at the dais. Head held high, Avery took measured steps through the room, taking time to smile and nod in greeting to those she passed. Feeling out of place was no excuse for rudeness.

At the baron's raised table, Avery settled into the chair Robert held out for her and offered thanks when he called for her meal to be brought from the kitchen.

"I have made my decision." Robert's gaze settled on her, thoughtful.

Her pulse ratcheted up at the dispassionate declaration. He was going to say he didn't want to marry her. She'd given him all he needed, so why would he choose to marry a stranger? She didn't want to. Calling this sham off was the right thing to do.

So why did her chest feel so tight?

Robert's face held no emotion. "The convent will offer you a life of protection and safety. If you—"

"*What?*" The word shot out of her mouth in a screech. A *convent?*

The room quieted, the occupants' eyes turning their direction. Robert lifted his eyebrows.

Avery lowered her voice and leaned close. "Are you kidding me? I'm not a nun. You can't seriously think I'll go to a convent. What happened to me staying here?"

Robert tapped a finger on the table, his expression unreadable. "The convent offers a quiet life of protection, should you wish it. If you so choose, I will pay the abbess a fine dowry for you to enjoy a comfortable life there."

Avery opened her mouth to protest further, but the slight way he lifted his hand silenced her.

"If you do not wish to enter the convent, then you are free to remain at Northwood. You may live out your days here under my protection."

Avery's shoulders relaxed. He'd been giving her a choice. Why in the heavens he thought she'd want to go to a convent, she had no clue. But she appreciated that he'd tried to give her options.

A girl of about twelve, who should have been in school, scampered up and placed a platter of cheese, cubed brown bread, and some kind of shriveled-looking fruit in front of Avery. She thanked the girl, who looked taken aback that Avery had spoken to her, before she hurried away.

"I can seek an arrangement with Lord de Wirth, so as not to burden you with a marriage." Robert plucked a piece of cheese from his plate and chewed.

Wait. What? "What are you talking about? You're just going to up and get engaged to someone else while you're already engaged to me?"

Why had she said that? Hadn't she already decided

she couldn't marry a stranger? The guy could marry someone else if he wanted to.

But still. Coldly tossing her aside to marry someone else without even giving this thing between them a chance irked. And there was a *thing*. She'd been kissed a few times in her life, but she'd never felt what she felt when Robert kissed her.

She was more than *irked*.

What happened to that peace she'd been feeling earlier? The rejection slipped fingers over her heart and squeezed.

A pained expression softened Robert's features. "Lady Avery. I will not deny that you have captured my interest, but I must think of my people."

"I thought I already handled that," Avery grumbled. She snapped her mouth shut. Why did she keep saying stupid stuff? *Desperate* was *not* the impression she wanted to make.

"Northwood needs an heir. That changes not."

She pushed a hunk of cheese around on her wooden plate. "And that has to happen right now?"

"Soon, yes."

Wow. "You're like, what? Twenty-five?"

"Seven and twenty, this past summer."

Avery lifted her eyebrows. "You know you have lots of time, right?" Even as she spoke, she wondered. The people in this time had much shorter life spans. Beatrice had said something about girls marrying around sixteen, some younger. Maybe that was because they only lived to their mid-fifties or something.

"I do not understand your meaning. I am lord of Northwood. It is my duty to produce an heir, or the line dies with me." He considered her, seeming truly confused as to why she didn't understand what he was talking about.

What a weird way to live. She heaved a sigh. She should let this go. Let the man marry whomever he wished. He'd given her permission to stay in the safety of the castle. In the meantime, she could try...

But she wasn't going home. If nothing else, she was sure of that.

So then what? Would she really let him marry someone else while her heart insisted that—given enough time with this rough-edged knight—he could be *the one*?

Avery lifted her chin. "No."

"No?" Robert twisted in his seat, fully looking at her.

"No, I don't want you to marry someone else." Her heart hammered, but she refused to leave anything unsaid. If this really was her second chance at life, then she wouldn't waste a single moment of it being a coward. "I want to at least give us a shot. Go on a few dates. See what happens. Can you give me that?"

Robert's eyes narrowed. "Your use of language often leaves me at a loss. You wish for us to wed?"

"Maybe. Someday." Avery shrugged. "Don't you want to see if what we have between us could be more?"

He shook his head. "I do not understand." A line formed between his eyebrows, and the intensity of his gaze drowned out the conversations around them. "What of your condition?"

Condition? Oh. Her CJD. "I think...well, I kind of think I don't have it anymore." Now he'd really think she was a nut. She'd better hurry and get the explanation out before he decided she needed to go to the convent after all.

"I hadn't started to experience a whole lot of symptoms. Just enough for the doctors to do a ton of tests. Girls my age don't really get dementia, you know?" His expression said she was losing him again. "Anyway, at first I would forget things I should know. People's names. How to get home. Things like that. Sometimes I felt like I was in a fog." She lifted her palms. "Since I've been here, all of that is gone. Part of the miracle, I guess."

"You have received a miracle?"

Avery pursed her lips. "I think so."

Robert shifted in his seat. "'Tis as the priest said."

"What priest?"

Lacing his fingers together, Robert stared at the tabletop. "When I was at prayers in the chapel, Father Ivan came to me claiming the Lord said unto him that I should look for a miracle to be bestowed at Christmas."

Avery laid her hand on his arm, and his gaze shot to hers. "I don't know if your miracle is the same as mine, but I believe I got one. I hope you do too."

Robert turned to his food without a word and started eating.

Avery sat back. That was it? So much for thinking they were sharing a moment. That man. They hadn't even come to a decision as far as this awkward "define the relationship" talk went.

Anger boiled up inside, and she shoved a hunk of thick brown bread into her mouth. She'd been rejected before, but the dismissal from this caveman really took the cake. Did he not give a single thought to other people's feelings?

"Very well." Robert gave a curt nod, dropping his eating knife with an air of finality. "It will be as you say."

"What will be as I say?"

"The banns will remain. In one week we will decide if you and I will wed. I will inform Lord de Wirth of your wishes, and he and I will make alternative arrangements regarding his daughter ere they depart. 'Tis a good plan, Lady Avery."

A good plan? Did he seriously just say she had one week to convince him to marry her or he would go on to plan B?

Where he already had a woman waiting in the

wings?

What was this? The medieval season of *The Bachelor*?

Lady Avery seemed upset, though Robert could not fathom why. He guided her down the long hall on the way to the chapel, their next stop in the walk through the castle. A walk she no longer seemed interested in taking.

She'd devised a wise plan. Due to her generosity, he did not need to wed her, leaving her the option to decide if she wished to marry him or live her days as a spinster under his care.

Though what if she later wished to marry another? The thought rankled, though he could not fault her. She'd made clear her desire to wed out of affection, the same reason she'd gifted his people with her wealth. For that, he would forever be grateful, and she could live as ward of Northwood for as long as she liked. If the time came when she wished to wed another, he would make arrangements on her behalf to the best of his ability.

The lady's touch was the barest feather upon his arm, cold and distant in comparison to the warm way she'd felt in his arms. The memory stirred him. If she truly was healed of her ailment, then they could proceed to the vows. She would be able to rear his children with a sound mind. And yet she had gifted him with a week to judge her capabilities while understanding his need to secure other arrangements.

Her repeated generosity heightened his affections, which continued to grow the longer he shared her company.

At the end of the hallway, Robert opened the door to the castle's chapel and led Lady Avery within.

He gestured toward the table set with a golden cross at the fore of the room. "You may make use of the altar whenever you need."

Avery eyed him and gave a small nod. "Okay. Thanks."

Before she could move forward, Robert gathered her hands. "What vexes you, Lady Avery? Do you not wish to see the castle any longer?"

"Vexes me? You mean you really don't know?" She turned her face up to him, anger in her tone but pain in her eyes. Had he said something amiss?

"Seriously. You know nothing about women." Avery huffed and pulled her hands from his grasp. "Did you really think I wouldn't be upset that you want to be engaged to two women at once?"

"Engaged?"

She crossed her arms over her bosom. "Intended to be wed. Honestly. Who do you think I am? Some puppy at your heels willing to compete with another woman for your attention?" She lifted her chin. "I'll be no man's second fiddle."

Robert ignored her strange phrases, dismissing them as a misunderstanding between their languages and not as a sign of her losing her wits. "You are offended with me seeking arrangements with Lord de Wirth? Why?"

"Good heavens. Really?" She speared him with sharp eyes, but her wrath did nothing to untangle his confusion.

Such interactions seemed to be weaving a pattern, one where she became increasingly angry, and he became increasingly confused. Was this what a marriage to Lady Avery would look like? He took a step back from her, refusing to repeat himself.

"Ugh." She threw out her hands in annoyance. "Let me try to say this in a way you will understand. Where I come from, it's our custom that a man entertains only *one* woman at a time. It's highly disrespectful to enter…*arrangements* with more than one lady."

Understanding dawned. He bowed. "My deepest apologies. I meant you no disrespect. I thought only to speak to the baron while he was near. No arrangements will be made until you and I decide if we shall honor the banns."

Her expression eased, and she regarded him for a long moment, judging, he thought, if he spoke true. "I guess you can't really call the guy. Communication must take forever here."

Robert contemplated her meaning. "Sending missives in winter to his castle takes a measure of time, yes. Though you are correct. I should wait until this matter is settled."

Avery gifted him with a smile. "Thank you. I would appreciate that."

He bowed again. Never had he seen a woman demand respect the way a man would. His appreciation of her fortitude grew. The woman would gift a husband with strong sons to be sure. "It will be as you say."

The pronouncement pleased her, and the hornet she'd once again become softened into a butterfly.

He looked around the chapel, an idea forming. "Shall we pray together? Perhaps the Lord will grant us wisdom in this regard."

Lips parting slightly, Avery gave a slow nod of consent. He led her to the altar, where they both kneeled.

As he took her hand, a feeling of rightness washed over him. She would have her week.

But he already had his answer.

Eleven

"He's set his mind to wooing you, that 'tis what." Sarah stretched her hands toward the fireplace in the grand hall, the sounds of bustling servants creating a din in the background. "Otherwise, he would never have ordered such a strange request."

Avery watched as castle folk carted in wagonloads of evergreen branches, bits of snow falling on the stone floors in clumps. All of this hubbub because she'd said she missed having Christmas decorations? The visiting nobles had departed two days before, and in the time since, she'd spent nearly every waking hour with Robert. They'd talked about everything and nothing. He'd explained his culture, as she'd tried to explain hers in as simple terms as possible.

Sarah sighed. "You know they will all have to be replaced. 'Tis far too early." Her tone held notes of both chiding and amusement. "Christmas is yet a fortnight away."

"Back home, people put out decorations right after

Thanksgiving. Well, actually, a lot of them start way earlier." Avery shrugged, lifting the heavy cloak thing Robert called a mantle on her shoulders. "The greenery makes the winter more festive."

A boy scurried by with a handful of holly leaves. Sarah laughed. "It does indeed. What is Thanksgiving?"

Explaining the pilgrims and Abraham Lincoln's Civil War holiday proclamation would only cause confusion, so Avery skipped to the heart of the celebration. "It's a day we set aside for feasting, to give thanks to God for all He has provided for us throughout the year. We do this in November."

"A fine idea." Sarah turned her back to the warmth in the fireplace. "Perhaps this is a tradition you can bring to us as well."

A Thanksgiving feast? She could invite all the castle people and the villagers, make it a grand event where the regular people could enjoy a big party as a thanks for all their hard work. Excitement stirred within her. She wouldn't lack for purpose. The castle presented many—though somewhat unconventional—opportunities to make use of her skills. With so many people living here, she would be event planning throughout the year.

"As lady, you will command the castle servants, and Robert will see that your wishes are done. I think he will agree to this giving of thanks day." Sarah watched with keen eyes as the workers carried out their tasks. Who did all the planning now? Would she be taking Sarah's job from her?

"And what about you?"

"Me, Lady Avery? I will step down from running my brother's household once he is wed." Before Avery formulated a response, she continued. "Worry not. I will be glad of it. 'Twas my duty after Mother's death, but I will not lament passing the role to my brother's wife."

Avery considered the girl. Woman, really. She might still be in her teens, but she was more mature than most women ten years her senior back in Avery's time. "I'd appreciate your help learning how the castle is run, if you don't mind. I have some experience, but I'm not sure how well my ways are going to translate."

A gleam entered Sarah's eye. "You've made your choice then?"

"Uh…no." Just because she wanted to know what running a castle this size would require didn't mean she'd decided to marry the baron.

Did it? She certainly stepped right into filling the role—part of it anyway. Heavens, she'd only been at Northwood a week. How did one's life change so dramatically in such a short period of time? Without her phone or the internet, time felt slower. That week seemed to stretch longer.

Avery shrugged. "I'm taking in all the information I can in order to make the best decision."

"Hmm." Sarah gave a coy smile. "As you say. Though I do not understand what makes you hesitate. I have seen the way the two of you regard one another. God has blessed you with a connection already, and you've not even wed. Is that not what women dream of?"

An undercurrent flowed through the words. "Is that what *you* dream of?"

Color bloomed on Sarah's face. "I have brought this matter to my brother. He has not yet made a decision."

"Wait. You mean Robert gets to choose who you marry?"

Sarah tilted her head to one side. The motion reminded Avery of a puppy who'd heard a strange noise. "Of course. Why would this not be so? He is the last remaining man of our family. The responsibility falls to him."

Oh boy. "What if you don't like who he picks?"

Sarah shook her head as though Avery's concerns were unfounded. "My brother cares for me. He will not make a bad match. Sir Robert will consider my wishes, along with the characteristics of any man he has in mind for me. He will make sure I am secure."

Wow. Avery had trusted her father entirely, but would she have wanted him to pick out a husband for her? The way these people thought felt completely foreign. "Do you already have someone in mind?"

Sarah dipped her chin. "Aye. My request is for a landless knight. This will not bring wealth to my family and will cause me to remain within Northwood. 'Tis much to ask. My brother is considering my choice against what is good for all of us."

For Sarah's sake, Avery hoped Robert let the girl marry the guy she loved. She still wasn't on board with this entire "marry someone for what money they bring to the table" thing. At least since she'd already given Robert all that jewelry, if she did end up marrying him, she could rest assured that it would be because they had chosen one another, not because he'd married her for what he could get out of the deal.

"Where do you want the trees, milady?" Sir Galahad, the knight who had kept guard over her when she'd been confined to her room, stopped in front of them. Dressed in a fur-lined cloak that draped over his chain mail, he looked as if he'd stepped right off a King Arthur movie set.

"Trees? As in plural?" At his confused look, Avery shook her head. "How many trees did Sir Robert ask you to cut?"

"Ten, milady."

Ten? The man had them cut *ten* Christmas trees? Avery tried to conceal her surprise. "Let's space them out around the room. One on each side of the dais, then evenly apart down the walls here." She indicated the long walls covered in tapestries. "Be sure to stay away from the fireplaces, as that will dry them out too quickly." She tapped a finger on her chin, her party-planning instincts kicking in. "Oh. And find me ten pots as well, large enough for the trees to fit in."

"Pots, milady?" Sir Galahad's forehead scrunched.

"Yes. Put the trees in the pots and secure them with rope so they stay upright. Then have the squires fill the pots with water each day. This will keep the trees fresh for several weeks."

Sir Galahad looked doubtful but stepped back and bowed. "As you say, milady."

After the man retreated, Sarah clasped her on the arm. "An inspired idea, Lady Avery. Did you bring back this method from your kingdom?"

She'd have to have the whole *kingdom* talk with Sarah soon enough. But not right now. "That's how we keep the trees alive for so long back home, yes. Some people just use fake ones, though."

"Fake?"

"Not real. They are…" Avery waved her hand. "Never mind." There were so many differences, she'd never be able to explain plastic trees. "What do you decorate your trees with here in England?" No electric lights or glass balls, so what were they going to do to make them pretty?

"We have never brought trees inside the castle before." Sarah sounded amused. "'Tis yet another task my brother asked of his men despite the unusualness of the request. Today they are cutting trees rather than practicing at arms. They find this most strange."

From an objective standpoint, asking men to cut

down trees and bring them inside would sound like a crazy idea to people who'd never seen a Christmas tree. Warmth spread through her. Robert had done all of this for her. The gesture meant even more, given how other people would see her request.

She'd been around Robert enough to know that as lord of the castle, people followed his every command. But he also took leading them very seriously. She had no doubt that they all saw him bending to the will of someone they probably viewed as a crazy woman. For a medieval man, she couldn't think of a more romantic gesture than making himself seem a bit foolish for a woman.

"Aye. Wooing you for certain," Sarah said, as though reading her thoughts.

Avery couldn't help but chuckle. "I must admit he's doing a great job of it." A thought occurred. "In my country, we give our loved ones a gift on Christmas day. I would like to get something for him. What do you suggest?"

Sarah thought a moment. "He's mentioned having a new sword forged."

A sword wasn't exactly the romantic present she'd envisioned. "Maybe something a little more personal?"

A loud thump stole whatever answer Sarah might have come up with. Both women turned toward the main entrance into the hall, where men's agitated voices echoed. They exchanged a look. A moment later, the trunk of a massive tree, hoisted by several men, came into view. They grunted, pulling what had to be a twelve-foot-tall cedar—at least.

Avery rubbed her temple. When she'd told Sir Galahad to get pots, she hadn't been expecting a tree that massive. And they were bringing *ten*? She needed to stop this. Lifting her skirts, Avery hurried across the herb-scented rushes scattered on the floor to find Sir Galahad.

The man eyed her as she approached. "You are pleased, milady?"

"It is quite beautiful, yes." She gestured toward the tree. "Have you already cut the others?"

"Three so far, milady."

"That is enough. Please, don't cut more."

Sir Galahad frowned. "Milord said ten, so ten it shall be." His features said he would follow the orders, even if that meant trying to dig up a lake and bring that inside as well.

"Yes, of course. But I fear Ro—" She caught herself. "I fear milord has misunderstood my request. We have much smaller trees in my land. These in England are far grander."

This caused Sir Galahad to raise a hand and stop three knights from returning outside. The men paused near the doorway.

Taking that as a good sign, Avery continued. "Milord is most gracious." The weird way of speaking was starting to feel a little more familiar, and the people seemed to respond better to her when she talked that way. "And I'm most grateful for his generosity. However, I ask that you seek him out to explain that I did not know your English trees were so large. I don't wish to cause such labor for his men. Three of these grand trees is quite enough. Be assured that I am most pleased. There is no need for more." She took a breath, hoping the Shakespearean-play-sounding speech worked.

After a moment, Sir Galahad nodded, looking mollified. "I will speak with our lord."

She let out a breath. "Thank you." Poor guys. No wonder they'd looked so disgruntled.

The knight turned on his heel and barked orders at the three others lingering in the doorway to find pig troughs to put the giant trees in. Avery pressed her fingers to her lips. Three massive Christmas trees, held in pig troughs?

This would be the most interesting Christmas ever.

The woman had most assuredly vanquished his wits. Robert plucked a squirming hound from the litter and held it up to examine, feeling the fool. What woman wanted a hound? And was he truly considering letting this thing in the castle? He had a feeling she wouldn't be content with the creature lurking in the hall. Somehow, he had the distinct impression the lady would keep this dog in her chamber. He frowned at the furry whelp. Foolishness.

Yet when he'd asked her how to make her feel more comfortable at Northwood, she'd mentioned a dog. If a dog would make her feel protected, then he would yield to the request. At least until she felt safe enough with him.

"A good breed, milord." The farmer nodded toward the large mastiff sitting in the straw, watching Robert handle her pup. "She not be a hunter, aye, like the lords raise. But she will keep daughters safe, of that I am sure."

He could have taken a hound from the kennels, but he'd not give up one of their well-bred hunters for a lady's whim. He'd known royal ladies to fancy small French lap dogs. He had none of the delicate breed here. Besides, this one would offer protection. Once it reached size. The one watching him featured a massive square head and jowls that could sever a man's hand. He gave a nod.

"It is ready to wean?"

"Aye, milord."

Robert fished a coin out of the purse at his waist and held it out to the farmer.

The man's eyes widened. "You want them all, lord?"

He chuckled. "This one will be enough."

The farmer babbled his thanks, tucking the coin away inside his cloak.

Robert had much to do for the people, but for today he could lighten one man's burdens in exchange for a slobbering whelp he'd use to earn affections from a woman.

He held up the largest pup in the litter and examined his black face and floppy ears. "If the lady doesn't care for him, I wish to bring him in exchange for another." He considered the sharp-eyed mother. "And if she doesn't wish to wait for this fellow to age, then I will return for that one." He pointed toward the giant head of the dog watching him.

"Certainly, milord." The man hesitated. "But, if I may be so bold, a whelp is best. They pick their family young, and once they do, no man will get through him to cause that family any harm without taking the dog's life first." He grunted. "And this type don't give up their lives easy."

Robert nodded. As he'd thought. This hound would serve well as a protector for his lady. He thanked the farmer and returned to his horse, awkwardly holding the dog in one hand. The whelp squirmed, making Robert tighten his grip.

He found Sir Galahad waiting for him in the inner bailey a few moments later. The knight eyed the whelp but said nothing about it. "The lady says that ten trees are too many, milord. She says that our English trees are grand, and she expected ones much smaller. I told her you ordered ten, but she asks that I tell you she says three English trees are enough."

"Then so it shall be." Robert waved the man away. If she wanted three trees in the hall instead of ten, so much the better.

Sir Galahad turned and disappeared inside to carry out his orders. Robert followed more slowly. He'd been reckless, using her desire for festive decorations this many weeks prior to the Christmas celebration as a way to win her favor. But having chosen his bride, he would earn her consent in return. The thrill of doing so excited him more than when she'd first accepted the arrangement for his protection. Perhaps she had been right. Looking to form a bond out of shared affection prior to speaking vows awakened an excitement within him.

Offering her the safety of his keep as freely as she had offered him her dowry felt right. He would win her. And if still she chose to live here without becoming the lady of Northwood, then he would honor that wish as well. But her refusal would not come because he had failed to show her that he was worthy of her affections.

He found Lady Avery in his hall, pointing and giving directions to the castle folk as they swarmed around her. She stepped into the role easily, speaking her orders with authority, yet kindness. The people hurried to do her bidding with smiles. He watched for a time, pleased with what he saw.

His sister approached and stopped at his side, curiosity on her lovely features. "A hound, brother?"

"Mastiff. The village folk use them for protection."

Sarah eyed the wiggling creature in his arms. "Why is it in the hall?" Before he could answer, Sarah laughed. "Lady Avery wished it? Truly, the lady has captured you."

"I do not wish to see her go to another."

"You could have demanded her to wed you or be sent to the convent if she refused. Instead, here you are with trees in the hall and a dirty bit of fur in your arms."

Robert grunted, words failing him. His sister had cut right to the heart of the matter.

"Ah, she has spotted you, my dear lord brother, and this way comes." She leaned closer. "Tell me, what thinks you of this woodland scene she has created in your castle?"

Truly, he did not know what to think of the greenery Lady Avery was directing the servants to spread across nearly every flat surface. Though he had to admit, he found the scent of cedar pleasing.

She approached quickly, her eyes wide and excited. "Oh! A puppy!"

The joy on her face brought a smile, and he held the whelp out. "For you, my lady. A protector, as you requested."

"What?" She reached for the animal even as she

asked, laughing when the dog wiggled in her arms and licked her face. "You brought me a dog?" The weight landed in her arms. "Oh. You're a big fellow, aren't you?"

"Aye. He will grow large and strong so that you may feel protected."

Moisture glimmered in her eyes. "You want me to feel safe here."

"You have my castle, my men, and now even this hound all sworn to see you safe, Lady Avery." He would lay down his life for her as well, were the need to come. As he stared at her, he sensed she knew that as well.

Water leaked from the corner of her eye the way it had for his mother that time he'd returned from his time of fostering as a squire with a bolt of fine French cloth. He'd missed her and had purchased the cloth in her honor. He hoped Lady Avery's tear bespoke of the same appreciation his mother's had.

"That is so sweet of you. Thank you." She snuggled the whelp close. "We'll have to come up with a name for you, won't we, big boy?"

A dirty animal in his home, yet her pleasure brought him the same. He caught his sister watching and schooled what must have been a broad smile. She leaned close. "The lady's heart is won. And to think, you did it with a whelp." She patted his arm. "Sir Henry accomplished such with a rose."

The words slammed into him. He turned to face his

sister. "I have thought on the matter. If you wish to live here at Northwood and wed a landless knight, I shall not deny you this request. I will be pleased to keep you close."

Sarah sucked in a breath and squeezed his arm.

"What?" Lady Avery stepped closer, struggling with the pup who now thought licking her face to be a game. "What happened?"

"Sir Robert has agreed to my request of husband." Sarah's face glowed with joy.

A good choice. And he would see that Sir Henry gave his sister every honor she deserved. With the couple residing under his roof, he could better judge how well the man treated her. Not that he expected anything but the best from Sir Henry.

Having lost the rest of his family, seeing his sister rear one of her own here at Northwood greatly pleased him. More—her children and his would bring much laughter and joy to this hall.

Lady Avery looked to Robert, a smile brightening her face further. "That's great!" She gave him an approving nod that should not have made him feel like a squire who'd performed a task well and had earned his lord's favor, and yet did. She turned back to Sarah. "I'm so glad you're staying." She swung her gaze back to him. "And that your brother realizes that love is what's most important."

What did she mean by that? Something in her gaze

played with him, teasing. Did she mean she had come to love him, even before they wed? Surely that meant she had made her decision.

The whelp suddenly jumped from her arms and hit the ground, rolling into a heap. Lady Avery yelped and reached for it, but the pup was faster than it appeared. Big paws slid through the rushes as it darted for a serving girl with a pitcher of water.

"Grab him!" Lady Avery shouted, dashing away.

Robert groaned, chastising himself for his foolishness even as he gave chase.

Twelve

*A*very paced in her chamber, kicking herb-scented rushes out from under her feet. Dawn cast silvery light through the wavy glass covering her window. Below, she could already hear horses whinnying and people moving around outside in the inner bailey. There would be no breakfasts in the hall now that the guests had all gone. Lora and Beatrice had already headed to the kitchen to fetch Avery a "morn repast."

Avery ran her fingers down the gown she'd chosen. She'd discovered that emerald and pale green were the colors for the house of Northwood. The fact that she'd chosen this particular gown spoke to her subconscious decision. Still. She had to be logical. Several of the dresses she now owned were in shades of green. The choice didn't mean anything. Not really. Did it?

Today she had to give Robert her answer. To decide if she would wed the baron of Northwood and become lady of this castle. Crazy. Marrying a man she'd only just met. Becoming some kind of baroness. Everything from the crown to the castle felt like something out of a dream.

If she said no, she would have to watch Robert marry someone else. Watch another woman move into his solar. Run his castle.

Have his children.

Why did the idea cause such an ache within her? Pangs of jealousy over the threat of another woman made no sense. She should let him marry a woman from his own time.

But would that woman know that under Robert's rough exterior lived a tender man who'd brought her the ball of fur curled sleeping in the middle of her bed? Or would another woman marry him just because it gave her a title and position? Would this unknown lady love Robert?

Avery pulled in a deep breath. Did *she* love Robert?

Despite what the man did to her insides, he'd walled himself off from something very important. She wasn't from this time, a fact he seemed determined to ignore, and something she had to settle before she could let herself consider a future with him. She needed him to believe her. Only then would she feel as though they had a solid foundation of trust.

She watched the sleeping puppy that brought her such joy curled in the very center of her bed. The darling had slept close to her, gifting the comfort that only a pet could bring.

Lora had been horrified last night when Avery had put the pup on the blankets. Apparently, inside dogs were not a thing. Except, she'd learned, if a lord let his hunting hounds into the hall during evening meals to feed on scraps.

Dogs were not to be seen in bed chambers. And they most *certainly* did not sleep in the middle of a lady's coverlet. Avery chuckled. Both girls had been rather displeased when their lady had insisted on going downstairs in the middle of the night to take the dog outside on a bathroom break.

Though not as displeased as the knights on duty. Or the cook. But that had been because the little guy thought roosting chickens would make wonderful midnight playmates. There'd been feathers, shouts, men with swords, and a rather rousing commotion that had seen much of the castle staff stumbling around in the dark. Avery had found the situation quite funny. The knights on duty, however, had not.

She'd warned the highest-ranking knight to expect her again tonight. He'd been disgruntled but had muttered a "yes, milady" anyway.

The puppy yawned, his long pink tongue lolling over his teeth. He stretched, and then, spotting Avery, jumped down from the bed with a yip. The door opened, and Lora bustled in, a large tray in her hands, Beatrice on her heels. The two girls twittered about something as they entered.

Long ears swinging, the puppy stuck his nose in the air, sniffing wildly. He bounded in their direction, his big paws slapping on the floor as he darted around the bed.

Uh-oh. "Lora! Watch—"

Lora squealed. The tray in her hands launched into the air. Honeyed milk, bits of bread, and a few pieces of cheese flew toward the ceiling. Beatrice yelled at the dog as his front paws landed on her legs, knocking her off balance.

Avery froze as the pewter pitcher in Beatrice's hands crashed onto the floor.

Beatrice pointed a finger at the puppy bounding around at her feet, happily snatching up the scattered contents of Avery's breakfast. "Hound! This will not do. Not do!"

Avery withheld a laugh as she hefted the pup, his weight already nearly thirty pounds. She wouldn't be able to lift him much longer. "I'm sorry, Bee. He does need a bit of training."

The young woman thrust her hands on her hips. "A lady's chamber is not a place for a hound. You should—" Her face suddenly paled, and she dropped into a curtsy. "Forgive me."

The laughter burst out of Avery now. "Oh, come on. You don't have to do that. You can be mad that the dog tripped Lora and made you drop breakfast. I get it." The dog squirmed in her arms, making Avery struggle to hang on. "I think he's hungry. And probably needs to go out." Potty training was especially difficult when one had to lug a thirty-pound weight through a castle.

"I did bring him a scrap of meat." Lora huffed as she gathered the food from the floor. "A hound in the bedchamber," she grumbled under her breath. "Whoever heard of such?"

Avery chuckled. "It won't be so bad when he's older." The pup squirmed with more vigor, and she grunted. "I better take him out before we have something worse than milk to clean."

Beatrice started to rise, her expression clear that she agreed.

Avery shook her head. "You two stay. I know how to get down there now. I'll be back in a bit."

By the time Avery made it all the way to the kitchen, the muscles in her arms burned, and the dog seemed as unhappy as she. "You're going to need a leash, boy. And soon."

The kitchen swarmed with the smells of roasting meat and watered-down ale as the servants prepared for the day. Avery practiced the names of the people she'd met, puffing out greetings as she lugged her puppy through the massive space. Women peeled potatoes and purple carrots, diced onions, and chopped dried herbs. They all watched her, some with judgmental glances and others with amused whispers.

Finally, she made it to the small enclosed yard and

set the puppy in the cold, wet grass. He immediately made a series of circles and did his business. She gave him a bit of privacy and surveyed the area. Chicken coops lined one wall, the fowl still nestled on their perches, save for one rooster, which eyed the puppy with suspicion.

She really needed to give him a name. He couldn't be more than two months old, yet he was already massive. She'd seen a mastiff at a dog park once. That fellow had to have been two hundred pounds. "He couldn't have gotten me a poodle?"

"You are not pleased?"

The sound of Robert's voice had her wheeling around. She placed a hand to her thudding heart. How had he managed to sneak up on her with all that chain mail and those thick boots?

"Sir Robert. You startled me."

"Apologies, Lady Avery." He leaned to look past her at the puppy, who had locked eyes with the rooster. "Perhaps you should dissuade him from testing out the bite of those talons."

She scrambled after the dog and hefted him up again. He twisted in her arms to lick her face, and she tried to angle away.

"Afore long, you'll not be able to lift him." Robert clasped his hands behind his back. "We do not have ladies' lap dogs in Northwood, but I shall fetch you one in London if you so wish."

"No, I'm already attached to this big baby." She set him down again, and he pounced on a patch of slushy snow. Avery shivered, suddenly aware of the deep chill of a December morning. Why hadn't she grabbed that thick fur cloak Lora had given her?

As though reading her thoughts, Robert unclasped the cloak around his shoulders and swung it around her. The weight settled, bringing with it a delicious warmth.

"Thanks." She snuggled in the mantle, bits of the fur at the collar tickling her cheek. "You're right. I won't be able to carry him much longer." A thought occurred. "Do you have a craftsman who works with leather?"

"Aye."

"Can I ask him to make something for me?"

"As lady of this castle, you may have anything you wish." His face remained passive, but she caught the undercurrent of his words. As *lady of the castle*. If she chose to marry him.

She stared at him. Nervousness fluttered through her and drained the moisture from her mouth. It was too soon. Too fast. She needed to tell him no. Let him go. For some unfathomable reason, she couldn't.

"Have you decided on a name?" He changed the subject, giving her a blessed reprieve.

Avery let out a breath. "He's going to be big. Really big. Like a tank."

"Tank?"

She regarded him, deciding now was a good time to

revisit the whole I'm-from-the-future conversation. "It is a motorized vehicle armored for war."

A flicker passed over his face, but she couldn't pin down the thought behind it. "You wish to name your whelp after something for war?" He watched the puppy bound around the yard, thankfully away from the chickens.

Nose to the ground, the pup pushed bits of wet snow clinging to the grass out of his way before digging with reckless abandon.

Avery laughed. "I've got it. Dozer. Big and pushy." She shrugged. "It fits." She waited for Robert to ask what the word meant, but after several moments of silence, she tugged her attention from the puppy to meet his gaze. "Do you believe me?"

That flicker went over his face again. A momentary tightening around his eyes before his face turned stony again. "There is much that is lost in the exchange of languages."

"That's not it." Avery stepped closer. "I've come to accept that I'll live out my life in this time. I need you to accept that this time is not the one I come from."

His shoulders stiffened, creating strain along the muscles in his neck. He closed what little distance remained between them. "Careful of how you speak. Many will think you mad. A baron's wife *cannot* be mad." The strain in his voice gave her pause.

"And you care what others say?" She scoffed. "I

didn't think you the type." She swiveled to move away.

Robert caught her arm. "Play not games with me, Lady Avery. You are not without wits. You know what dangers such talk will create. And I cannot leave you knowing you could come to harm."

"Leave? Where are you going?"

"A lord does not always keep residence in his castle. We have taken a great victory over France, but I know not how long this peace will last. Come spring, King Edward may yet call on us again. I will not leave for war knowing my lady could come to harm."

The news sank into her. She knew the man was a warrior. Not only was she considering marrying a stranger, but a soldier. Looking at him in his chain mail, sword at his hip, he embodied a man poised for a fight.

Fierceness filled his gaze. He would protect her. No matter what that meant. Something inside her broke free. A longing to mean that much to someone. How long had it been since someone cared so intensely for her? Not since losing her parents had she embraced the comfort of having others to lean on. God had given her a fresh start. Someone to love who would put her best interests first. In light of that, making others accept her origins was unimportant. "I…understand. I'll not speak of it."

Tension drained from his expression, and he cupped his palm against her cheek. The rough skin of his hand gently caressed. "Let us not worry over things to come. I am here this day. As are you. 'Tis all we can ask for."

The words sank in. Hadn't her diagnosis given her a new perspective? Life was full of unexpected twists and turns. No one knew what a day might hold. She could only live in the moments granted to her.

Could she really marry this man? Take such a leap? Let herself dive off a cliff and hope he would catch her? Protect her and cherish her? Marriage meant commitment, a complete giving of oneself to another. To do that, there had to be trust. Without the foundation of trust, nothing more could grow.

"I'd still like to know that you believe me, even if I never breathe a word of where I came from to anyone else."

Robert cupped the back of her neck and drew her closer. "I believe you are a miracle sent to me. I believe you come from a faraway place, filled with many things I do not understand."

He hadn't said he believed she came from the future. But...maybe that didn't matter. She could have said she'd come from another planet, and it probably wouldn't have sounded any more alien to him. He'd come halfway. She could meet him there.

Avery nodded. "That's good enough." A smile lifted her lips. "Thank you."

He touched his forehead to hers. His words came low and deep. "I vow unto you my life, Lady Avery of a

156

faraway and future land."

The breath froze in her chest. He didn't say that he loved her. Yet somehow, the words he'd used touched deeper. He'd promised her his life, something she did not take lightly. He meant he would die protecting her. He would live honoring her. Avery moved closer, pressing the warmth of her cloak against the cold of his chain mail.

Words forced their way through the thickness in her throat. "I never expected to marry a man I've only known a few days."

Robert chuckled. "More than a sennight since you fell from the sky."

"I did not—" The teasing in his voice registered, and she laughed. "Fine. A week then. How is it that I can feel so much for you so fast? Do you think…?" She hesitated. Did she dare speak her fears out loud?

Robert waited. Patient. Content to let her sort through her thoughts. His fingers gently caressed the back of her head, the sweetness of the touch tempting her heart to let go of all logic.

"Do you think these feelings will last?" What if she got caught up in all the craziness of the situation, but after they got to know one another, that initial infatuation fizzled?

"I keep my vows, Lady Avery." His voice grew deep, nearly ominous.

What did that have to do with feelings?

"I have vowed my life unto you. I will vow my love unto you if you become my wife. No matter what feelings come with the day, the vows remain."

Avery swallowed, considering the weight of his words. They may not always have fluttery feelings. But this man—honorable and trustworthy—promised that he would love her anyway.

Commitment saturated his eyes, and she knew.

"Yes, Robert."

He pulled back, questions on his face.

"I choose to marry you. I would like to be your wife and vow to honor you for the rest of my earthly days."

A smile erupted on his lips a moment before he gathered her close and kissed her until he'd vanquished any lingering doubts that would dare defy him.

Thirteen

"To arms! To arms!"

Avery awoke with a start. Somewhere outside, a bell clanged, the frantic toll breaching the thick stone walls. What in the world? Men's voices shouted beyond her bedroom door. Heavy footsteps pounded a harried rhythm down the hall.

Beatrice snatched open the heavy curtain surrounding Avery's bed. Dozer yelped, then let out a low growl. Beatrice ignored the dog's empty threat. "Hurry, milady." She tugged the covers from Avery's body. The disgruntled puppy yelped as he rolled off the bed.

"What's happening?" Avery's pulse skittered as she scrambled from the bed. Shadows still clung to the room in thick clusters. Gray morning light attempted to breach the windows, but had little effect.

"We are under attack!" Lora burst through the door. Her eyes landed on Avery, who still stood dumbfounded in her nightgown. Lora rushed to the wardrobe and snatched out a clean dress then threw it in Avery's direction. "Hurry, milady. We must go."

"Go? Go where?" *Under attack.* The words finally cut through her muddled senses.

Robert would fight.

Avery snagged the blue fabric from the air and tugged it on over her nightdress. No time to worry with proper layers and perfectly tied ribbons.

"I don't know, milady," Lora fetched Avery's shoes. "The lord wants you in the hall."

"Why?" A tinge of worry snaked through her stomach. Hadn't Robert said something about brigands?

"They are his orders, milady," Beatrice inserted. "Best we be about them."

Lora grabbed the heavy winter cloak from a hook near the smoldering fireplace. They wouldn't leave the castle, would they?

Avery didn't bother to wash up, clean her teeth, or brush her hair. Suddenly, hygiene didn't seem so urgent. Lora helped tie one side of the strings on the gown while Avery's trembling fingers dealt with the other.

Dozer sniffed the rushes, and then tinkled on the floor.

No one cared.

They rushed for the door. Avery scooped the pup into her arms and settled his growing weight against her chest. Her hair fell free around her shoulders, and Dozer took the opportunity to nip at the strands. Men in full knight's armor pounded down the hallway, shouting orders. The cacophony echoed off the stone walls.

Brigands.

At the gates.

Demands.

Bits of shouted words snagged Avery's attention as she followed the knights to reach the stairs. She nearly collided with Sarah on the first step.

"What's happening?" Avery shifted the puppy in her arms, he the only one of them unconcerned with the tension permeating the air.

Sarah gripped Avery's fingers. "Men are at the gates. They are calling for Sir Robert with demands."

"Brigands?"

"I know not." Sarah tugged on her arm. "We must hurry."

The puppy jostled in her arms, his whines protesting her haste. But she didn't dare put him down with so many armored men running around. She needed a crate. Another thing she would have to request be made. Once they survived this attack.

Avery stopped at the bottom of the stairs. What did she think she would do? Carry Dozer until the threat passed? "Hold on. I need to go back."

"For what?" Sarah's wide-eyed gaze darted toward the hall, where Robert's voice boomed orders.

"Dozer. I shouldn't have brought him. But…well, he needs somewhere to be."

Beatrice appeared at Avery's side in that uncanny way she had of always being where she was needed. "Give him here. I will take him to the yard and see that one of the squires secures him."

She didn't know what exactly Beatrice meant by that, but she'd simply have to trust her. She handed off the pup, who immediately struggled to escape. Avery patted his head. "Good boy. I'll be back for you soon."

Beatrice scuttled away, the pup's two hind legs swinging against her hip.

Avery followed Sarah and Lora into the main hall. She'd barely stepped foot inside the room when Robert's voice cut through the murmur of knights and castle folk.

"Lady Avery! To me!"

Men parted in her path, and she rushed for Robert. "Are you all right? What's happening?" She stopped cold several paces from him, the stern look on his face reminding her once again of the beast she'd thought had turned into her handsome prince days ago.

"What knowledge have you of this?"

"Me?" Avery shook her head. "I don't know what you're talking about."

"Men ravaged one of the villages during the night. A messenger stands at the gate, and fifty men this way come."

The dangerous edge to his voice rooted Avery to the floor. "Robert. Why would I know anything about men at the gate?"

His gaze bore into her with the intensity of a man determined to root out a lie. "Because the messenger demands your return."

"Return?" Fear shot cold spikes through her center. "Return where?"

Robert growled low. "I told you I will not play games. Do these men come from your kingdom?"

"And I told *you*," she hissed, glancing at the men gathering in clusters around the room. "I don't have a kingdom. I'm here completely alone from…you know." Her voice strained. "I thought you believed me."

His gaze raked over her, a mixture of fury and pain warring in his eyes. "You will come."

Avery's heart stilled. Was he about to turn her over to a band of lawless men? She opened her mouth to protest, but the look on his face left no room for argument. Avery lifted her chin. Fine. She would go. But only to prove she wasn't who these guys were after. There had to be some mistake.

The holes in her memory about how she'd arrived at Northwood squeezed her stomach. She hadn't caused some kind of issue without knowing it, had she? Had anything happened between when she'd gotten ready for bed at a seaside Victorian inn and when she'd awakened in Robert's garden the night of the ball?

Another thought jolted her. Surely the time warp hadn't created an entire history for her. No way. There wouldn't really be a kingdom out there somewhere missing its princess.

Right?

Lora draped the heavy wool cloak over Avery's shoulders, and Avery pulled the comfort of it close. Head held high, Avery kept pace with Robert's long strides, her features under iron tight control even as her insides roiled.

She and Robert snaked through the inner bailey, where men notched arrows into bows and gathered in lines, swords at the ready. Should the gates open, they would pour out like a death wave onto whoever dared step foot on Northwood grounds.

Overhead, leaden clouds hung low, drooping to-ward the earth with the weight of snow. Maybe the morning was more spent than she'd realized. Life without clocks could be a bit disorienting. Her mind scrambled in every direction in an attempt to stave off the fear that pushed cold daggers into her chest.

Robert would not hand her over to these men to avoid a fight.

He wouldn't.

Would he?

He'd made it abundantly clear that his people came first. And like a naïve fool, she'd already given him all of the jewels. She was at his mercy. Avery forced the worry away. No. She had seen his desire to protect her. She would trust him. She dared a glance at his stony profile.

No emotion cut through the hard lines of his face. No hint that he felt conflicted over what to do.

Whatever he'd decided, his mind was already made. No matter how much she told herself that should bring comfort, worry still insisted on souring her stomach.

They reached a set of stairs that led up the wall surrounding the outer bailey. At the top, winds whipped at Avery's cloak and sent her hair flying in a mad tornado around her shoulders. She grabbed the loose strands and stuffed them underneath the hood, hiding most of her face beneath the fur's warmth.

Robert positioned himself like a statue at the wall of the outer bailey looking down at two men on horseback in the field just outside the gate.

"What business do you seek with Lady Avery?" Robert's voice boomed, startling her.

Instinctively, she took a step closer to him. She could trust him. She could. That didn't stop her from pleading her case. "Please, Sir Robert." Avery looked up at him, but he refused to meet her gaze. "I haven't done anything to bring trouble here." She bit her lower lip. "At least, not to my knowledge."

He ignored her.

Below, the two knights silently sat atop massive warhorses. Snowflakes drifted down, attempting to coat the ominous scene before her in a blanket of redeeming white.

The knight to the right nudged his mount forward.

He wore a suit of armor that, until recently, Avery had only seen on television. The weight of the metal didn't seem to bother the giant horse, the creature garbed in its own breastplate with a metal carapace covering the length of its mane. The armor covered the beast's forehead, making it look almost like a cyborg of horseflesh and metal.

"Release the princess unto her people, and no more harm will come to your lands." The man gestured toward Avery as his mount pawed the ground.

Robert growled. "I will not. If it is a fight you came for, then a fight you shall have."

Avery tensed. Robert would fight for her. But not if she could do anything to stop it.

Avery leaned over the balustrade and raised her voice. "Who are you? What do you want with me?"

Robert spat something under his breath, but Avery ignored him, her gaze on the man below.

"We are your people, Princess Avery of Gardenia. This man has stolen you from us, and your father demands your return!"

The shout carried on the frozen air, slamming into Avery with a start. Her…father? Could somehow—in this crazy mixed-up situation—her parents be lost in the Middle Ages as well? Had Dad woken up as a king and now searched for her? Had the time warp actually been the creation of an entirely new life for all of them?

Even as the thought caused an ache in her chest,

she pushed the notion aside. No. If Dad had been here, he would have come for her himself. He would not have sent armed men.

"You lie!" Her voice cracked with the declaration, the illogical ache for the knight's claim to be true squeezing her heart until she felt as though it might disintegrate within her.

Robert took her arm and nudged her behind him. "You will leave these lands or face my men. Lady Avery is to be my bride. She stays with me."

"Turn over the jewels that belong to her kingdom, and you can keep the wench!" The voice came from the other man, thick with disdain.

The first knight turned to him and said something too low for Avery to hear. He moved his warhorse forward, closer to the castle and away from the other knight.

Avery breathed deeply, the cold air searing her lungs. If she'd had a sliver of hope about the truth of the first man's words, the latest demand convinced her. There was no way her father would have demanded the jewels instead of her. Whoever these men were, what they really wanted was the crown Avery had gifted to Robert's people.

Robert tensed, likely thinking the same thing. The second knight had given away their true purpose.

Robert positioned himself more fully in front of her so that Avery could no longer see the men below. He shouted something in what Avery recognized as French at the two knights and then whirled around. He looped his arm around her shoulders, urging her toward the stairs back down to the bailey. "To your chamber."

"Robert." Breathless, Avery allowed him to hasten her from the upper wall as hooves pounded away behind them. "Robert! Stop."

He paused in the center of the stairs, his eyes hard.

"I don't know what they're doing, but there's no way those men came from my father. My father died years ago. And even if by some miracle he were here, he would have come for me himself. And he would *never* ask for money over me.

The words caused a flicker in those icy eyes, but only for an instant. He gave a tight nod, though she couldn't tell if she had convinced him. "To your chamber."

At the bottom of the stairs he turned away, shouting for his horse and yelling at men to ready their swords. The portcullis began to grind open. An instant later, Robert disappeared into the chaos.

Avery stood dumbfounded in the outer bailey while men rushed around her. She should get to her room. To safety. Even as the thought urged her to flee, Avery remained rooted to the spot. Snow fell on the clanging armor of men readying for battle. Energy crackled in the air. The grinding of the portcullis came to a halt, and men rushed out. First those on massive warhorses, then others on foot.

Pressed against the wall, Avery watched it all. A medieval battle was about to unfold around Northwood Castle. But why? Who were those men, and why had they attacked Northwood's village? What did any of that have to do with her?

Nothing about the situation made sense. She was missing something.

The last of the men pushed through the gate, leaving a strange quiet and emptiness behind them. The portcullis began its slow grind back toward the ground. Avery sucked in a breath. Robert had said for her to return to her room, but she wouldn't be able to watch the battle from there. She couldn't hide away, not knowing how he fared.

She eyed the upper wall. Men lined the top, bows at the ready. She wouldn't be able to stand among them. Her gaze swept over the upper rooms of the castle with its nearly opaque windows. Where could she—?

A blur of fur rocketed around the corner of the castle and through the middle of the outer bailey.

Dozer!

Avery pushed herself off the wall, nearly tripping on her long cloak. Oh no. The puppy ran straight toward the portcullis! Avery chased after him, shouting his name. The dog didn't slow. He bounded through the lowering gate, a fierce little bark daring anyone to stop him.

He would be trampled.

Before she could think better of it, Avery dashed through the bailey. She slid underneath the portcullis just before the metal slammed to the ground.

Fourteen

*B*lood boiled through Robert's veins. He pushed his heels into Cesar, his destrier already pulling away from the men at his back. The horse's hooves ate up the snowy ground until they were far enough away from the castle that Robert drew up.

They would fight on the open ground here, just inside the range of the longbows on top of the castle wall. People from the villages and those usually journeying inside the castle for their daily work had all been ushered through the rear gates, guarded by a segment of his men-at-arms. Once they had seen the castle folk safely enclosed in the hall, they would join the battle here.

If only fifty men had come, as Robert's scout had claimed, his men would withstand this battle. He waited, the cold wind knifing against his armor yet failing to chill him.

If Avery had wished to go with them, he may have considered letting her, which was why he had risked taking her to the wall. But Avery had not recognized them. Called them liars. Robert believed her. Whoever these men were, they were not Avery's people. Therefore, they would meet the swords of Northwood.

His knights drew up their horses around him. Waiting. Cesar pawed the frozen ground, his body tense with readiness.

A shout rose from the distance. Pounding hooves vibrated over the ground, coursing through Robert and bringing the familiar taste of battle to his tongue. His senses heightened as his focus narrowed in on the mounted enemies emerging from the swirling snow. Their forms appeared as mist before clearing into a band of armored brigands without colors or banners.

He'd fought on French soil in a dozen battles larger than this. Had killed many, wounded even more. Had watched his father and his brothers die. He'd fought for his king and his country. Yet in all the battles he had fought, none had been on his lands. None had been for his lady. And none would cost him as much.

Robert breathed deeply, gazing through the snow struggling to obscure the field in front of him. He lifted his hand, signaling his knights to hold fast. The enemy must come into range of the bows before his men moved to face them.

Cesar's breath billowed in front of them, mingling with snow. The pounding hooves grew closer, the men's armor more distinct. Horses whinnied behind him. Still, he held.

Horses broke through the haze. Men's shouts mingled with the falling snow. Their blood would soon color the ground. For Northwood. For Avery. He would spill as much as he needed to keep these men from stealing what he held dear.

Closer.

The horses' breath billowed white smoke. The men atop them raised their swords.

Robert dropped his arm.

A whistle of arrows sailed overhead, slamming into the brigands and the ground in front of him, sending horses rearing. His men gave up a cry, and their warhorses lurched forward.

Hooves, shields, and swords all collided with a teeth-jarring force. Cesar reared, capturing unmounted men beneath his giant hooves. Robert slashed, sending one brigand crumbling to the bite of his sword even as he kicked out from the other side of the saddle, keeping a man from catching Cesar's flanks. He jumped from the saddle and landed in the center of the fray.

Thrust, block, parry. He fell into the rhythm of the sword he'd known all his life. A dance of blood and death. A necessary evil to keep safe those he loved. They came for her, and thus forfeited their own lives.

He crossed swords with one man, then another as each fell to the swing of his blade. Around him, the battle raged, his men valiantly fighting for the honor and safety of Northwood. Robert heaved a breath, his focus widening to the enemies now scattered around him. Thirty, he guessed, and no more.

Blood coated shields and dripped from swords, speckling the white snow that tried to cover the mark of men's sins beneath its purity.

Something was wrong. A brigand lunged from Robert's left and Robert swung his sword to clash with his enemy's. Whatever was amiss, he didn't have time to consider it now.

A shout warned him of a man at his rear, and Robert turned in enough time to block the blow. His sword rang out in a rhythm against the blackguards who came for him, his steel biting into one man after another.

Swords hit, and a jolt crashed through Robert's arm. A brigand shouted at Robert as he lunged again. Rage boiled, forcing the pain from Robert's body. There was only the fight. This man would not take from him. He would give nothing. With a feral growl, Robert sprang forward, his sword finding purchase. The brigand fell, his body crashing into the slick snow.

A sharp sting of pain sliced through Robert's lower leg, causing him to stumble. The man at his front, a sneering brute with a bulbous nose, grinned as Robert lost his footing. He raised his sword. Robert dove, rolling to his side.

The brute's sword hit empty air, causing him to lose his own balance. An attacker at Robert's rear stabbed at him, narrowly missing. His legs churned against the wet earth, trying to regain footing.

A sword swung for his head.

Metal clanged on metal, and the brute grunted. Sir Henry's sword bore down on the other man, and the brigand slipped in the snow. Sir Henry finished him.

Robert gave the man who would soon be his brother-in-law a grateful nod. Blood ran down the back of Robert's leg, but he ignored the pain and forced his body to stand.

Around him, his men held the ground and pushed the brigands back. Bodies lay in heaps in the snow, the majority belonging to the enemy.

"We've taken them, milord!" Sir Henry's shout drew Robert's attention.

The man had taken two prisoners. The rest lay dead.

Robert scanned the fallen. Too few. He glanced toward the trees, but he did not think any had fled. He tensed, waiting for another band of men to come for them during the vulnerable moments just after a battle they thought they'd won.

No more men came from the trees. The arrows had ceased their flight from the castle walls.

His instincts warned something wasn't right. Sir Willis was a reliable scout. He'd said fifty.

Why come for him with lesser numbers? Robert had had them two to one, and in short order, they had fallen to his knights' swords. At fifty, they would have been more evenly matched.

Realization slammed into him like a flight of arrows. Too few men. No men on the castle walls. Fear pumped through him.

"We ride!" Robert dashed for Cesar and launched himself into the saddle.

Fifty men, and only thirty were dead or captured.

His men protecting the rear of the castle had never joined the battle.

As he'd fought here in the field, the enemy had snaked around behind him.

She could reach him. Avery dove for the puppy just as an explosion of arrows erupted from the top of the castle. For a moment, the sky blackened as the arrows took flight and sailed overhead like a flock of death. Transfixed, Avery followed their path through the air, horrified as the projectiles slammed into a pack of men on horseback. Two sides clashed, and the sound of chaos washed over her, even at this distance.

She couldn't make out which side belonged to which as men melded together in a writhing mass of destruction. Her heart hammered. Robert.

Please, let him be okay.

Something brushed her leg, and she yelped, heart

leaping into her throat. "Oh. Dozer." She reached down and hefted the dog. "You shouldn't be out here."

The puppy frantically licked her face, then turned his nose up to where another *thwang* announced the release of more arrows. She tucked the puppy under her cloak and hurried back toward the gate. Her feet slid in the freshly fallen snow, and she crashed down on her hip. Pain rocketed through her thigh, and Dozer whimpered.

"Sorry, boy." Fear pounded in a heavy drumbeat though her veins, but she forced herself to remain calm. She needed to get back inside the castle. Find Sarah and Beatrice and Lora. Being surrounded by friends would quiet the panic struggling to capture her. They would know what to do.

This was all her fault.

Out in that field, men were fighting to the death. Fighting because of her. Or the jewels she'd been sent here with.

Why? Why did You do this?

Men shouted as they clashed, and the sounds of death ripped through what should have been a beautiful snowfall and tainted the air with death. Avery strained to see through the swirling white to find Robert, but it was impossible to distinguish him from the other hazy forms.

I'm so sorry.

Her chest squeezed. The cold wind slapped against

her face, snow mingling with her tears. This horrible, dangerous century chewed people up. What would happen to Northwood if Robert died? Would those men come and take her? There were no laws here. No police force and court system. If Robert lost, there would be no one else to stop them.

Avery prayed Robert would survive unharmed.

He wouldn't want you out here, endangering what he could be dying to protect.

Her senses snapped out of the fog of fear freezing her to the ground and riveting her eyes on the battle. She had to get hold of herself. Get inside to safety. There was nothing she could do out here in the snow except get herself killed.

Move!

Avery forced her mind to focus and her feet to move. She hefted Dozer on her hip and bounded for the portcullis.

"Open the gate!" She tucked the dog against her and rattled the frozen metal. "Open the gate!" No guards appeared.

She backed up and tilted her head toward the upper wall. Where had all those men with bows gone?

"Hey! Let me in!" Avery scrambled back to the gate and pushed her face into the space between the iron bars, trying to see anyone within the bailey. Shouldn't there be someone watching the gate? Dread wormed through her stomach, making her feel sick.

Shouts and the distinct clang of swords sounded from beyond the outer bailey, from the wrong direction.

Enemies had gotten inside.

Avery pressed herself against the stone in the small alcove of the gate. There were brigands inside the castle. Looking for her? Her lungs heaved, pushing out puffs of white smoke. What should she do now? She could run for the battle raging across the field. Warn Robert.

No. She'd never make it there without being seen, and nearing the fighting men would only give the brigands opportunity to grab her. Avery squeezed her eyes closed. She could make for the back gate, try to get inside through the kitchen. Maybe she could sneak past—

Dozer growled.

Avery's heart skipped, and her eyes flew open. The scream lodged in her throat as a man in bloody armor lunged for her.

Fifteen

Avery came to with a start. She placed a hand to her throbbing temple. Murky memories surfaced. The man coming for her. The blow to the side of her head. Dozer.

What had happened to him?

She groaned and rolled over on her side. What had happened to *her*? Avery spread her fingers, feeling a thin mattress stuffed with straw that scratched at her. Opening her eyes, she willed them to adjust to the dark. She could scarcely see the bed, let alone anything else. But the space was silent except for the sounds of her breathing. She didn't think anyone shared the dark, though she couldn't make out much more than the wooden wall behind her and the musty mattress on the dirt floor.

Panic tried to claw up her throat, but she forced herself to stay calm. More memories returned. The rough men. Grabbing her. Taking her. She'd fought. But struggling had only gotten her a pounding headache and bruising along her arms. If she wanted to escape, she would need to think.

Muffled voices drifted on the frozen night. Men. She could hear them through the wall. Avery pressed her ear to where a crack seeped winter air.

"…can't keep her here long." The gruff voice belonged to the man who'd assaulted her. The one who had easily overpowered her and slung her over his shoulder.

She'd landed a few good blows to his neck before he'd smacked her in the head and rendered her senseless. If she'd remained conscious, maybe she could have picked up a clue as to where they had taken her. How long had she been out?

"You know the orders. We wait until Northwood responds."

Avery pressed her ear harder against the crack. Robert. Did he know they had taken her? Were they trying to ransom the jewels? Her heart sank. Even if he had shown tenderness toward her and made all those vows, Robert would never choose her life over the people of his barony. In some sense, she couldn't begrudge the man his loyalty to those who depended on him. One life for many wasn't logical. Still, that didn't make what the decision would cost her any easier to bear.

What would these men do with her if Robert didn't pay the ransom? She shuddered as possibilities assailed her. If they hadn't meant her harm, they certainly wouldn't have injured her already. Avery rubbed her cold wrists. At least they hadn't tied her up.

She couldn't afford to sit around and wait for a man to decide her fate. Gathering as much courage as she could muster, Avery pushed off the bed and eased along the wall, fingers splayed to feel her way around the room. As far as she could tell, only the mattress occupied the small space. No tables, chairs, or other furniture. Nothing she could conceivably use as a weapon. Her only option would be trying to escape.

But then she would be outside, where she would most likely get lost and freeze to death. One problem at a time. At least she had a chance of survival against the elements. Hypothermia would be a better way to die than at the hands of ruthless barbarians.

The voices of her captors faded as she inched her way farther around the small room, finally coming to a door. Pushing down on the latch, she tried to contain the whimper of disappointment at discovering what she already knew.

Locked.

Desperation surged through her, demanding she rattle the door. Break the lock. Escape. Avery sucked in a lungful of air, held it, and let it out slowly. Panicking wouldn't get her anywhere. She had to think.

The voices moved closer. A thump. A door opening and closing nearby. Footsteps.

"Think I'll have a bit of fun while we wait." The dark laughter following the words sent Avery's heart into a wild gallop.

No.

The other man said something she couldn't make out over the pounding in her ears. Whatever it was, the first man growled a foul reply. Avery scooted against the wall, tucking herself behind the door.

The latch rattled. Creaked. Slowly, the door moved closer. Avery held her breath. One hulking shadow, then another, stepped inside the room. A faint light from the other room spilled across the floor just enough to turn her world from pitch black to shades of gray. Both men paused, probing the shadows. Looking for her.

Now!

Avery darted around the massive form of the hulking man in the doorway and burst through to the next room. As the man whirled to grab her, Avery slammed the door on him and dropped the locking bar into place. She dashed through a small living space bathed in lamplight. She tripped on the leg of a chair and slammed into a table.

Her side screamed in pain. She couldn't stop. One of the men roared. The loud crack of wood splintering filled her with terror. How long would the simple latch hold them?

Avery rocketed forward, eyes darting across the room. There. Another door. Praying this one wouldn't also be locked, Avery lunged. The latch moved in her hand. Frigid air greeted her, blasting her face with freedom. Another crack of wood sounded behind her. Her trick had only bought her a few precious moments. She prayed they would be enough. She burst out into the night.

Starlight and a half moon illuminated the snow-covered ground, a landscape of cold beauty that would betray her every move and hinder each step.

Her cloak snagged on something and wrenched her backward. She screamed.

Struggling with all her might, she tore at the strings at her throat, refusing to give up her forward momentum. The leather strands broke. She stumbled forward, sliding and filling her shoe with snow. Avery regained her footing and churned her legs forward, pumping her arms.

Avery sprinted, hoping her body would resurrect the strength from when she'd trained for that half marathon the year before. She pushed hard, careening through the darkness and heading for the cover of trees beyond the small clearing. Shadows seemed to reach for her. Limbs of sinister trees ripped her clothes.

Blindly, Avery plunged into the woods, trying to put as much distance between herself and her captors as she could. Her chest heaved. Her feet caught on roots. Her steps faltered as she slid in the snow. Every misstep could cost her life. She pushed forward, not daring to

184

slow even as pain from the cold bit into her feet.

Avery kept sprinting, dodging the shadowy forms of branches and tree trunks. She ran until her lungs threatened to burst and then pushed herself more. No arms reached for her. No shouts gave away the positions of the men who most surely would be chasing her by now.

In the back of her mind, a voice of reason told her she could be running in circles. Taking herself toward the tiny cabin. Or into the path of the men she was trying to avoid. She had to find somewhere to hide. A place to disappear. To rest. Crashing through the woods would make her easy to track even if the darkness covered her footprints in the snow. Thankfully, this deep in the woods the thinner layer wouldn't as easily give her away.

Help me.

Avery slowed her steps, straining to listen for her captors. An owl screeched, nearly making her heart explode. She whispered prayers over and over, asking that somehow God would shield her movements from evil men and provide her with a place to hide.

She picked her way through thickening underbrush. At least the changing terrain meant she hadn't back-tracked. Nothing she could do about leaving prints in the snow, but maybe they wouldn't be able to find them in the dark.

Avery moved toward what looked like a flat rock

jutting out of the side of a hill. A tree grew on top of the stone, roots reaching over and around. Would there be enough space for her to squeeze under there?

What she wouldn't give for her phone. She couldn't call 911 but at least she would have a flashlight app. Some creature probably already called this hole a home and wouldn't welcome her intrusion. At best, the space would be infested with spiders and creepy crawlers. Avery shivered, the frigid wind cutting through the gown she'd thrown over her nightdress. Had that really only been this morning? She already felt as though she'd lived a year since staying the night at a mysterious inn in Ocean Springs.

Something snapped behind her. Avery froze. A twig? Under the boot of one of those men? She looked behind her but couldn't make out anything in the shadows.

Please.

The single word encompassed every hope and fear that swirled in her chest. God help her.

Avery scrambled beneath the rock, pulling her skirts in tight behind her. She curled into a ball on the damp earth just as footsteps burst through the trees.

He had failed her. Robert ground his teeth in frustration

as darkness fell on Northwood Castle. He'd promised to protect her.

His castle, his men. Himself.

None had been enough. Robert cradled Avery's whelp over one arm as he stalked through the inner bailey.

The dog had been crazed, yapping outside the front castle gates. He ran in circles, barking fiercely. Robert had needed to pick him up to get him back inside the gates. Once inside, the animal had followed Robert around the grounds, nose to the stones.

Looking for his mistress.

Had he been older, the hound may have been of some help. Naught but a whelp, the dog could do little to aid in the search. When he'd finally lain down and whined, Robert lifted him and let the pup rest along the length of his forearm.

Seeing one of Avery's maids upon the front castle steps, Robert limped in her direction. The wound on his leg had seeped too much, but he would have to see it tended later. He handed the whelp over to the maid's care. The young woman hefted the dog's weight, her eyes asking questions. At the set of his features, she had her answer. Avery had not been found. Worry flooded her young face as she turned and hurried inside.

He'd arrived back at the castle just as his men finished off the last of the intruders. They had broken in, looking for Avery, her dowry, or both. He'd lost five knights, three squires and a kitchen servant in the melee. Seventeen brigands lay dead in the outer bailey. They'd searched every inch of the castle and had not found more. Nor had they discovered his missing lady.

Robert's boots slammed against the stone floor as he burst into the hall, sending servants scattering. Two ragged men stood before the dais, arms bound and guarded by two of Robert's knights. Robert drew his sword, fury driving him. He pointed the tip at the hollow of the older enemy's throat.

"Where is she?" Voice low and full of danger, Robert fought to maintain control so as not to run this miscreant through before he could give up Avery's location.

The man's voice remained calm, his eyes steady. "I know not."

The tip of Robert's sword bit flesh, drawing a sliver of red. He did not want to kill this man, but he would if it meant finding Avery. "You attack my keep and steal my betrothed and you *know not?*"

Something in the man's eyes shifted. Slight. But enough. Robert pulled back on the blade, giving but a hair's breadth between metal and skin. "You did not know she would be taken."

The man's mouth remained closed, but his eyes gave answer. Whatever orders this man had been given, they had not set well with him. The suspicion about who had been behind this attack took root.

Robert lowered the sword. "I would have your name."

The man kept Robert's gaze, his mannerism betraying him for more than a brigand. "Sir Thomas."

A knight. Robert clenched his teeth, suspicions solidifying into fury at this betrayal. "Who sent you?"

Conflict flickered in Sir Thomas's eyes.

"A man loyal to his master is honorable." Robert stepped close, studying him. "Yet if the lord he follows shows no honor…" he trailed off, watching the knight.

The younger of the two captives shook his head at his senior, warning in his gaze. Youth would render the boy, barely old enough to have earned his spurs, reckless. Robert would fare better with the older man's wisdom. Robert gestured to his knights. "Take this one below. I will come to the dungeon once I finish here."

The two knights led the prisoner away, leaving Robert with the older enemy knight. Robert sheathed his sword. Suspicion had wound through him as he'd searched the castle for Avery. The men who'd attacked were English. Therefore, someone who had known of the arrival of the princess at Northwood Castle had sought to take the jewels.

Now he knew who. The same man who had warned of foreign brigands that had never been found. Robert gripped his sword hilt. "There is no dishonor in choosing not to follow a lord who sends his men unto evil."

The knight shook his head, sending bloodied bits of fair hair across his forehead. "A knight who betrays his lord has no place in service."

"He may serve here." The words came before Robert had given them much thought. A knight who betrayed his lord may well betray the next. Yet a man who was strong enough to stand against wrongdoing might be worth having. Time would tell.

Sir Thomas studied Robert, searching his face for any sign of deception. He would find none.

"A knight disloyal for selfish reasons is not worthy. But an honorable man who speaks against what he knows is wrong is valuable." Robert stepped closer. "You are Wirth's man."

Surprise widened the knight's eyes for only an instant, but it was enough to confirm Robert's suspicions.

He clenched his fists and blew out a breath in an attempt to control his anger at his ally's betrayal.

He would have entered into arrangements with Sir Alfred de Wirth if Avery had not shown up that night. A small barony, the union with neighboring Northwood would have strengthened Wirth's holdings. Since Sir Alfred had only one living child, a daughter, if she were to wed Robert, then her son would inherit both Wirth and Northwood lands. Avery's coming had cost Wirth much. But he still had a lovely daughter. He could have found another arrangement without seeking war with Northwood. Perhaps Robert's wavering with his marriage arrangements had angered the man, angered him enough to make him devise betrayal to soothe his pride.

"He knew I could not give up the jewels. Why take her?" Robert's voice held an edge that knifed through the room, carrying easily on the empty air. Did Wirth think that, if he would not give up the jewels and if Lady Avery disappeared, he would then be forced to marry Lady Aldreda?

The knight hesitated a moment. "I knew of no orders to take her, milord."

Rage boiled. "Yet you were ordered to attack!"

"Aye. To distract while a small group took the back gates. They were sent for the jewels."

Robert paced. "Then why the men at the gates demanding her return?"

"I know not."

A ploy to distract him and continue the ruse that men from her kingdom sought her return? Wirth had no way of knowing Avery had not come from a foreign kingdom at all. Mayhap he thought Robert would never know who had betrayed him, laying the blame at the feet of a foreign king.

"Though if our men took her," the knight said slowly, "then my only notion as to where they would hide her would be the old midwife's hovel. 'Tis close enough, and secluded."

Robert stared at the knight for a long moment. "Sir

Henry!" A few seconds later, his most trusted man appeared at his side. He'd known Sir Henry would not be far. "Take Sir Thomas below. Once this matter is settled with Lord de Wirth, he and I shall come to terms."

Sir Thomas nodded his thanks as Sir Henry led him away. Alone, Robert stalked in front of the hearth, the pain in his leg demanding the surgeon's care. He longed to ignore the wound and the night and go in search of his bride.

But he could not ride in this weather. The torches would not burn long. The moon did not give enough light by which to see, and the driving snow would cause them to lose their way within the first league of Northwood. Sir Robert silently cursed the storm forcing him to wait until dawn. If any man put a hand on her...

Robert clenched his teeth. He would not sleep this night. Instead, he turned toward the chapel. He'd spend the hours in prayer, begging God to protect her when he could not.

Sixteen

So very cold.

Avery's teeth chattered, snapping against one another painfully. Hard earth pressed against her ear and cheek. Avery could scarcely feel anything beyond the bone-deep ache that permeated her body. Where was she...? Her mind moved slowly, as though her very thoughts tried to freeze.

Simple commands felt difficult. What had happened? *Think.* The battle. Dozer. Two men with evil intentions. She'd run into the night. Fear poked through the fog in her brain, bringing her fully awake. Avery's eyes snapped open.

The men. She'd stayed still in her hiding place, barely daring to breathe, until the footsteps had finally passed by. For hours she'd waited, fear as cold as the night stinging her veins. But no one had found her.

Somehow, between disjointed prayers and snatches of fitful sleep, she'd survived the night tucked literally between a rock and a hard place. Relief trickled through her, and her eyes drifted closed. She was safe.

A nagging sense of urgency warned she must not go back to sleep. She had to get up.

Avery pried her eyes open and willed herself to focus. Light seeped through the roots dangling over her hiding place, letting in slices of inviting yellow. The sunlight called to her, promising warmth. Reason pushed to the surface of her languid thoughts. If she didn't move, hypothermia would claim her. She had to get her blood flowing.

Move. Think.

Avery groaned, her body protesting the curled position. She moved her toes, stiff and painful, then her ankles. As best she could in the tight confines, she worked her hands down her arms, stimulating her fingers and numb skin. Finally, she risked prying back the dangling roots to get a view of her surroundings. The world beyond sparkled white. Trees wore gowns of shimmering snow, their green trimmings hanging with the weight.

Avery wiggled out of the small hole that had shielded her from much of the frigid environment as well as from the prying eyes of her captors. She stood, regaining feeling in her limbs and searching for monstrous men to come charging out of the woods. Birds chirped, flitting from one branch to another and sprinkling snow.

No sign of the men who had taken her. More snow

had fallen sometime during the long night, covering any tracks. The glittering forest around her revealed no signs of the men looking for her. Were they gone? Had she truly escaped?

Sunlight drifted through the trees, dappling the ground in patches.

Avery turned slowly. She had no idea where to go. But she couldn't stay here. Praying for wisdom and a heavy dose of good fortune, she stepped into the woods.

Another league, then he would have her. Robert pushed Cesar harder, though the warhorse already plunged through the drifts at a reckless gallop. Behind him, the mounts of his men thundered across treacherous ground. Curse Wirth for his greed.

Knights and destriers alike wore the colors of Northwood, his banner flying in the wind. If he did not find Avery in the place Sir Thomas mentioned, then he would ride to Wirth Castle, and they would know Robert came for war. Beside him, the knight who had given up his master's plan rode with the stoic posture of a man caught in a difficult circumstance. If his information now proved true—and did not lead Robert into an ambush—then Robert would have mercy on Sir

Thomas and offer him a place at Northwood.

They thundered across snow-laden fields, pushing into Wirth territory. Sir Thomas gestured east, and they veered toward the edge of the woods. He made no effort to hide his approach. If Wirth's men wanted to come for him, let them come. He feared not battle this day. The horses dodged through the trees, barely slowing to navigate the slippery ground and low limbs.

A few moments later at Sir Thomas's nod, Robert reined Cesar to a stop in a small clearing. They'd found the right place. Apprehension swirled through him. The small hovel, the only building in the meadow, remained quiet. No horses stood hobbled nearby. No smoke rose from the chimney.

Robert raised his hand to his men, signaling caution. He dropped to the ground and unsheathed his sword. The snow that had gathered on the doorstep remained free of footprints. If anyone had stayed the night, they'd done well to hide it.

Robert stalked to the thatched-roof structure that would do little to keep out the winter chill. He thrust his boot into the door, and the wood splintered and caved.

He waited a breath, but no shouts arose and no swords came at him looking for blood. Worry clawed up his throat. If not here, then Avery had to be in Wirth castle. Would Robert have to lay siege to a man he'd once considered his ally?

The hinges groaned as Robert pushed himself inside, Sir Henry on his heels. Robert took in the room in a glance. Dirt floor. Peasant furniture. Cold hearth. In three strides he crossed the room to the only other door and shoved it open.

Empty.

Robert growled and spun on his heel. Back outside, he made for Sir Thomas, who looked displeased. Had he sent them in the wrong direction? Did he have a plan that laid a trap for—

Something caught on the toe of Robert's boot, and he looked down. Underneath a thick blanket of snow, a mound revealed a patch of dark fabric. He lifted the object, tugging it free from where the hem had tangled with the barren limbs of a thorny bush. His fingers clutched the fur lining as heat swarmed through him.

Avery's cloak.

She'd been here.

Avery pressed her back against the rough bark of a tree, fingers trembling. Thundering hooves crashed through the forest. Had they come back with more men to search for her? Would they find her? Take her?

She needed to run. Hide again. Hide. Yes. That was what she should do. No. No, it was too cold in there. Too small. But those men were dangerous, and...wait.

What if those were Robert's knights? Had they come for her? How? How did he find her?

She dared peeking around the side of the tree. Men on horseback darted through the woods at an alarming rate. She pulled her head back before one of them spotted her. How did those horses even fit between those trees? They were big horses. Like, super big. Guess they had to be, carrying knights in full-on armor.

Avery tried to focus. What was wrong with her? Her thoughts fuzzed at the edges, making everything difficult. She had to focus. *Focus!* Why did it have to be so cold? Her teeth slammed together, chattering no matter how hard she tried to make them stop.

These could be Robert's men. She had to look again.

Pressing her stomach to the bark, Avery slid one eye past the trunk just as the last horse snaked through the trees roughly twenty feet away. The creature wore all that silver armor. Why did a horse need knight's armor, anyway? Did they really have a problem with people stabbing horses?

She moved out from behind the tree. Honestly. These people. Kidnapping and horse stabbing. Fighting over some jewelry like a bunch of lawless—

No. Her thoughts were running away again. She let out a long breath that puffed from her nostrils in white smoke.

Think.

Other than the armor, the horse wore a blanket of dark green. The rider. *Look at the rider.* She peered at him as he disappeared through the underbrush. A green tunic covered his wide back. Avery gasped. Green meant Robert.

She reached toward the fleeing knight. A call lodged in her throat.

But what if another group of knights also had green for their house colors? How would she know? She might be calling out to the very villains looking to capture her. She pressed her lips together.

Avery curled her aching toes inside her thin shoes. She would have to take the risk. Sneak close enough to see if they were Robert's men. If not, well…well, she didn't know.

But if she stayed out in the cold any longer, she feared she wouldn't survive long enough to care which knights had come.

Robert approached Sir Thomas, who held his gaze.

"I am sorry, milord. I know not where else they may have taken her."

Robert studied the man, searching for deception. He found none. Avery had been here. Her cloak left outside did not bode well. He dug his fingers deep into the snow-crusted wool. If any man had laid a hand on her, he would—

Movement flickered in the woods. Robert drew his sword and motioned for his men to stand at ready. Silence fell thick as he waited, eyes searching the trees.

A flash of blue fabric swayed about ten paces deep in the shadows west of where his men remained mounted in the clearing. Whatever scout had come, Robert would run him down. Make the man tell him where Wirth had hidden Avery. The figure retreated. Rage pumped through Robert's innards, sending his training and caution scattering. The scout would not escape!

Sword drawn, Robert dashed into the woods. The figure darted away. A cry too shrill to be born of a man escaped as the small person stumbled. Flaxen hair whipped across a gown, and Robert's heart seized.

"Avery!"

The figure slowed. Turned, wide-eyed and filled with fear. She swayed. He dropped his sword and ran.

Her hand reached for him. Her eyes closed.

She crumpled to the earth before he could grab her.

"Avery!" Robert hit his knees and gathered her cold, still body in his arms.

Seventeen

Something cold pushed against her neck. Avery groaned and tried to roll away but found herself tightly ensconced in blankets. Her entire body ached. She shifted, partially waking enough to notice her surroundings. Except for the insistently cold, wet sensation at her throat, the rest of her body felt cocooned in blessed warmth. She moaned and snuggled deeper into the softness encasing her and sighed contentedly. Sleep was a beautiful thing.

"Avery?"

A man spoke her name with tenderness, coaxing her out of the sleep promising to shield her from the discomfort in her limbs. Flashes returned to her memory, determined to draw her out and make her face reality. She'd been so cold. Alone. Afraid. There had been men in the snow. Someone had come for her...

"Avery? Do you wake?"

Her hand lifted, and calloused fingers encased her palm. Warm lips caressed her skin.

Robert. He'd been there. In the snow. He'd come for her. Her eyes felt glued shut, but she forced them open. Robert's face swam into view. His hair hung limp over his brow, his cheeks unshaven. Intense blue eyes searched her face.

"Are you well?" Worry and tenderness filled each word as he gazed at her with open concern.

A section of her furry blanket shifted, and Dozer whimpered, his cold nose burrowing into her neck once more. Relief welled in her chest, and Avery chuckled even as her vision misted.

Home. She was home.

A tear leaked down the side of her cheek as she gave the dog a pat and focused on Robert. "You came for me."

His hold on her hand tightened. "Aye. Though I feared I had lost you to the cold. What happened?"

Avery sank her fingers into folds of fur at Dozer's neck. "A man. He…he grabbed me. I struggled, but he hit me and knocked me out. I woke up in a dark room." She closed her eyes, willing the fear she'd felt then not to well up now. "I heard them talking. One of them wanted to…" She clenched her teeth, and Robert let out a sound low in his throat. She opened her eyes and snagged his gaze. Fury burned behind his eyes, but his hold on her remained gentle. "When they opened the door, I escaped. I ran out into the woods."

Relief deflated the tension in his shoulders. "You

were unharmed."

Avery nodded. She didn't exactly feel *unharmed* by the terrifying situation, but she knew what he meant. "I found a place to hide. I'd lost my cloak, but by some miracle, I didn't freeze to death. When I came out in the morning, I saw men ride by. They wore green, so I followed to see if they were your knights."

A smile softened the hard lines of his face. "You did well." He lifted her hand to his lips again. "My brave lady. A miracle you are indeed." He leaned close, placing his forehead against hers. "I am blessed to have you returned to me."

She slipped her hand from his and placed her palm against his rough cheek. "How did you find me?"

"One of Wirth's knights told me where to look. When I found only your cloak at the hovel..." His words thickened. "I feared I had lost you."

The emotion in his voice churned her heart. She ran her fingers through his hair. Wirth's men. The baron whose daughter Robert would have wed if not for her. "I know you couldn't give them the jewels. The people need them."

He lifted his head away from her and searched her eyes. "God has had mercy on me, and I have both." He rubbed her cheek with his thumb, sending her pulse fluttering.

"I'm sorry, Robert. I didn't mean to cause you such trouble."

"Sir Alfred brought trouble when he thought to take the jewels for himself, thus putting me back in a position to seek a dowry."

Avery frowned. Realization sank in. "He came to steal the jewels. But when he failed to get them, he took me instead."

"Aye. Though he did not know I would discover who had sent those men."

If Wirth wanted to put Robert back into a position of needing a dowry, then he never intended to let Robert trade the jewels for her return. They would have killed her, even if Robert had handed the crown over.

"He thought he could send knights disguised as men from your land." A wry smile tilted one side of his mouth. "He knew not that your kingdom is not of this time, nor did he think one of his men would prove more honorable than he."

Oh boy. What a mess.

"Sir Alfred thought that without the jewels and without you, I would marry his daughter, giving him not only the union he desired, but your wealth as well." His gaze bore into hers. "He would have never returned you."

Avery nodded, having come to the same conclusion. She breathed deeply. "Thank you for coming to save me."

His voice hardened. "Now that you have awakened, I will ride for Wirth Castle. This betrayal will not go unpunished."

Her fingers clenched his hair, preventing him from pulling away. "No."

"No?" Robert's brows drew together. "He stole my betrothed and attacked my keep." He spoke as though she had not understood.

Avery shook her head, a tear leaking out. "It's my fault."

"Yours?" He drew back, studying her. "How can this be?"

"You told me to go back inside the castle." She swallowed when his eyes darkened. "But I stayed in the bailey. I was worried about you and I…" She shook her head. "They were closing the portcullis when Dozer ran past me. He must have escaped from Beatrice. He went under."

Robert groaned. "You left the safety of the castle for the sake of a whelp?"

Avery clutched a hand around the pup defensively. "He needed me."

After studying her a moment, Robert gave a nod as though deciding something. "Wirth started this war, and I shall see it finished." Fire crackled through his tone. "Your actions do not change his."

"No." She clutched him tightly. "You can't go after him."

His face clouded. "'Tis not your place to say if a man will ride to avenge—"

"*Please*, Robert." The pleading silenced him. "If you do this, men will die. *You* could die. Then what? I will be left here all alone."

"You misjudge my ability." His voice was low, dangerous.

Avery shook her head. "I do not. But it *is* a fight and you *could* die, no matter how good you are. And even if you don't, if you kill Lord de Wirth instead, then what? His people come for you and the cycle of revenge continues." She searched his face, begging him to understand. "Let it go. He lost. He didn't get the jewels, or me, or trick you into marrying his daughter. You know he cannot be trusted. Tell the king what he has done and let justice be handed out." She leaned forward. "But please, don't go looking for more trouble. Stay here. With me."

Robert considered her for a long moment. Finally, he let out a sigh she considered his acceptance of defeat. He gestured toward the pup between them.

"This was foolishness and could have cost your life." He clutched her chin, his expression serious. "'Tis only a dog. I would have gotten you another."

She lifted her chin even as he kept gentle pressure. "I don't want another dog. I want this one." She lifted her eyebrows, hope dropping her voice to nearly a whisper. "As I suspect you did not want another wife, but rather this one."

His eyes widened, and then he leaned back and let

out a deep laugh. He released her face and placed both hands on his knees, leaning away to settle into the chair positioned by her bed.

Avery's face heated. She'd meant that as a romantic gesture. Maybe a way to get him to confess that he cared for her.

Loved her.

Instead, he laughed at her as if she'd just said the stupidest thing in the world. Really. These people might throw marriage around like some kind of bargaining chip, but he didn't have to act like saying she was irreplaceable was a joke. Heat pulsed through her, pushing out any lingering aches from the cold.

He could laugh all he wanted. She knew her worth.

His sparkling eyes met hers, and he grinned. Actually grinned. Amazing how the full stretch of his mouth transformed his face. She chided herself for thinking about how handsome he looked while he treated her so dismissively.

"Aye, my lady. You are most correct."

Correct?

"Though I dare think that my affections for you far outweigh that which you feel for the hound." He eyed the creature contently stretched out along her side. He raised one eyebrow teasingly. "Though perhaps not."

Avery let the beginnings of a smile flicker over her lips.

Robert tapped a finger on the chair, serious once

more. "You are a brave one, risking your life for that which you love. Even if it be naught but a dog." He leaned forward. "The world best take care, for my lady bears the heart of a knight."

He dropped to one knee in front of her and took her hand. "Lady Avery of the future—fearless beauty that defies evil men—will you accept my love and this very day be my wife? I ask this of you not for your dowry nor to bestow on you the protection of my name, but because I have discovered that I cannot live a moment more without you by my side."

Avery's heart hammered. Again, he asked her to marry him. But this time...this time it was everything she'd dreamed of. Well, maybe not exactly. She'd never dreamed of a rugged knight proposing to her after she'd barely survived hypothermia because she'd been chasing a dog through the snow outside of a castle.

But the love shining in his eyes? The well of hope and happiness swelling within her? That part was even more than she'd imagined. Avery sat up and threw her arms around his neck.

"I love you, Sir Robert of Northwood."

His arm tightened around her. "And I you." His lips hovered over hers. "This means you consent?"

She laughed and pulled him tightly against her. "Yes, Sir Robert. Indeed, I do."

Eighteen

Christmas Eve, 1356

The great hall had been transformed into a Christmas wonderland. Avery drew in a deep breath of the herb-scented rushes and took mental stock one more time before her guests arrived. She'd never thought she would plan her own wedding celebration, but then God certainly had a way of giving the unexpected.

Robert, bless him, had ordered the castle folks to follow whatever strange, foreign customs his lady required. The hardest part for him had been waiting on the wedding, especially after she'd consented to marry him that very day after her ordeal. But she had wanted to do things right. At least, right to her own sensibilities. If she was going to jump into the deep end with this new life, holding on to a few of her own customs felt reasonable.

Medieval tradition said she and Robert would marry on the front steps of the chapel, but Avery wanted something a little different. Something very much like what now unfolded before her.

Two massive Christmas trees stood on either side of the raised dais. The table had been cleared away for the ceremony but would be brought back in time for the feast immediately following the wedding. She, Sarah, and the castle girls had spent hours laughing and talking in front of the fires these past several nights as they had strung garland. Avery smiled at their creations as she fingered a strand filled with shriveled berries. Poor Beatrice. The small orbs had been lovely yesterday, and the girl had been so proud of her contribution.

The trees held all manner of random objects children had delighted in collecting, tying the items with thongs of leather or bits of string before hanging them from the branches. She counted several smooth rocks, a couple of horseshoe nails, and even a small iron cross crafted by the blacksmith. His daughter, a dark-haired darling missing both front teeth, had presented her prize with such joy that Avery had requested her father also make stars. The blacksmith had been honored by the request, and now two matching stars crafted of thin bands of iron graced the crowns of both trees.

After several days of inviting the villagers and castle folk into the hall to help with the preparations, the festive spirit had taken hold. Laughter and joy had filled the giant space, making Avery feel at home in a way she'd never thought possible. Now, most of them had returned to their homes to ready themselves for the day's festivities. The quiet moments that followed felt somewhat surreal. In only a couple hours' time, she'd be a bride.

"Milady?"

Avery turned from her inspection of the Christmas tree to find the burly blacksmith smiling at her. "Hello, David. Are you and the family ready for the party?"

He offered a toothy grin as he bobbed his head. His curly hair had been freshly washed, and his eyes glimmered. "Eva and the girls are finishing their dresses." He gestured toward the doorway. "I've brought what you requested, milady."

Her gift for Robert. "Were you able to do the inscription?"

"Aye. Even had the priest come have a look. To be sure I had it right."

Her gift would be a bit unconventional, but unusual had become her normal. "Wonderful. Can I see it?"

She followed David outside to the inner bailey, where a cold wind danced with a few tiny snowflakes. Two young boys proudly held the gift between them.

Avery pressed her fingers to her lips. "It is perfect, David. You have done me a great service."

David beamed. "Thank you, milady."

The boys held a shield roughly two feet tall, shaped in the traditional triangle-like shape Avery had expected. The center held a finely crafted cross, painted white. On each side, the words of Psalm 18 graced the metal.

"Did Father Ivan object?" She didn't remember a lot about medieval history, but she was pretty sure priests frowned on translating the Bible from Latin.

"So long as the words are from our Lord, I see no reason not to use such in battle." Father Ivan's voice came from behind her, holding a note of humor. Avery turned toward the kindly priest and smiled. He gave the shield a nod. "A fine gift, milady."

The translation probably wasn't perfect, but Avery had done her best from her memory. She prayed the words would serve as a reminder if ever again Robert went into battle.

The Lord is my rock, and my fortress, and my deliverer; my God, my strength, in whom I will trust; my buckler, and the horn of my salvation, and my high tower. I will call upon the Lord, who is worthy to be praised: so shall I be saved from mine enemies.

She ran her fingers over the words. No matter what happened, the Lord would be their shield and their strength. "Squire, see that this gift is safely tucked away so that I may gift it to our lord after the wedding."

"Aye, milady," the older of the two boys said. A moment later, they hurried toward the castle doors.

Back inside the hall, Avery counted the benches ready to receive her wedding guests. Thankfully, she hadn't needed to bother with printing and mailing invitations. Every person in the barony knew they were welcome at the castle tonight to bear witness to the wedding of their lord and lady and then share in a night of Christmas festivities. Already, smells wafted from the kitchen, promising a grand celebration feast that Robert had been able to secure thanks to the jewelry Avery had brought and to the generosity of the people adding to the bounty. They had everything they needed, and everyone had been invited. Save for those she most wished to see.

"There you are!" Sarah hurried forward, her hand gesturing around the room. "All is finished here. Come. You must get ready."

Avery let her gaze roam over the room once more, satisfied with the results. Rather than a DJ, she would have three minstrels playing for their first dance—one she insisted they would share as a couple and *not* as a group. A sudden sadness welled in her, and she let out a long sigh. If only she could share a dance with Dad as well. See Mom's smile as she accepted her turn with her new son-in-law.

"Lady Avery?" Sarah frowned, concern etching the corners of her eyes. "Are you unwell?"

Avery swiped at a tear forming. "I wish my parents could be here."

A sorrowful smile touched Sarah's face, and she grasped Avery's hand. "Aye. 'Tis a hard thing. We must thank our Lord God for those still in our lives even as we remember those already gone. But our memories keep our loved ones close, yes? Even if they cannot be here."

Avery squeezed Sarah's hand. She and Robert would wish their parents could be here as well. They would always miss them. Avery would always wish Mom and Dad could see all the milestones in her life. Her wedding to an English baron. Grandchildren.

God's plans weren't always what one expected, which Avery was quite literally living proof of. Not only had He saved her from an early death in her own time, but the life He'd given her at Northwood went far beyond anything she could have imagined.

"Come." Sarah gently tugged on her arm. "We must get you ready." Excitement filled her tone, beckoning Avery to tuck away melancholy thoughts and embrace the moment. "You will be the most beautiful bride Northwood has ever seen."

Avery allowed her friend and almost sister to lead her away, smiling at the thought of wearing her princess dress one more time.

Why did he feel as though a downed stag thrashed within his chest? Robert shifted his feet on the raised dais, hoping the people gathered on the rows of benches down the length of the hall did not take note of his twitching. He cast a glance at Father Ivan, who stood calmly at the head of the room. Were all men this unsettled on their wedding day?

Avery had transformed the hall into something from a bard's tale. A wonderland forest. Green boughs graced nearly every surface around the room, and shiny objects hung from trees the inventive woman had somehow managed to keep alive thus far. He'd not been keen on the idea of waiting to speak their vows, but he had to admit she had given them a memory worth waiting for.

Never had he seen his people so joyous. Avery hadn't cared for any of the nobility to travel to see the beauty she'd created for their vows. Instead, she'd made sure that every soul residing within the bounds of Northwood knew they would be welcomed here this eve.

Candles flickered from dozens of stands all around the room, creating an enchanting glow. Of a sudden, the minstrels picked up their instruments and began playing a slow, melodious tune he'd not heard before. His gaze rested at the end of the long center aisle that led from the entrance of the hall to the dais.

A bark sounded, followed by two oversized paws bounding into the clear space between benches. If that hound—

The whelp stopped at a firm command from Avery's maid, dropping down to his stomach in what Robert could only describe as begrudging consent.

Avery had commissioned the leather smith to craft a harness that wrapped around the dog's chest, with a long lead attached at a ring situated between Dozer's shoulders. The contraption worked quite well, and the dog had been yielding to the training. Robert had often seen Avery walking the grounds, the hound secured at her side. He would prove a fine protector.

Dozer's ears perked up, and a moment later a vision of beauty captured Robert's senses.

Avery.

Dressed in the very gown she'd worn that first night, she glided into the room. All eyes turned to watch her as she neared. The dress draped over her shoulders, golden embroidery falling like sculpted icicles onto her upper arms. This time, she wore no crown. The emerald pendant that had once belonged to his mother and three generations of Northwood women before her rested at the hollow of Avery's throat.

On her head, a golden circlet encased a long veil covering the glory of her flaxen hair. His hands clenched, imagining the feel of the softness between his fingers. Her eyes sparkled as she joined him at the dais, God's own creation more radiant than any ornamentation man could have produced.

This ceremony was nothing like he'd expected. There had been no procession. No display of his wealth or places of honor given to the nobility. And he couldn't have chosen a ceremony more perfect.

She looked up at him, her smile radiant.

He leaned close. "You are most fetching, my love."

She opened her mouth to respond, but Father Ivan made a low clearing of his throat and gave an amused lift of his brows. Avery chuckled, her eyes speaking where lips need not. Already, they'd begun to share a language of looks and expressions between them.

Father Ivan lifted his hands, then proceeded to ask the marriage questions. Were they old enough to wed? Not related by blood? Had they properly published the banns? The questions were asked and answered for the benefit of the witnesses, Father Ivan himself already knowing each answer Robert would give.

Next, Father Ivan read out the details of the dowry, listing the crown jewels of the Kingdom of Gardenia. Robert then pulled a small purse from his side, handing the symbolic thirteen coins over to his bride. At the close of the ceremony, she would distribute them to the poor at her discretion, signifying her authority to make financial decisions on Robert's behalf.

"It is time for the vows." Father Ivan gestured to Robert to plight his troth.

"Lady Avery." He raised his voice so that all might hear his pledge. "This day I vow unto you my word to keep you and you alone in bed and at table, for better or worse, and in sickness and in health, until death parts us." He pulled the ring he'd had fashioned for his bride from the pouch at his side and held the offering up to her. His voice lowered for her alone. "Made from the jewels of your crown, to symbolize the joining of our two lives, customs, and futures."

"Oh, Robert," Avery whispered. "It's beautiful."

The large, rectangular sapphire nestled in a bed of smaller diamonds and amethysts. An heirloom to pass down to their children and their children's children. He handed the ring to Father Ivan, who blessed it before handing the item back to Robert.

Robert slipped the golden band onto Avery's first finger. "In the name of the Father." He moved the ring onto her second finger. "And the Son." He positioned the ring to her third finger, pleased it fit correctly. "And of the Holy Ghost. With this ring, I thee wed." The ring rested at the base of her finger, glittering in the candlelight.

Avery smiled up at him, her eyes luminous. Though not tradition for a bride to speak at the ceremony, Lady Avery was anything but conventional. Her voice was melodious as she pledged herself unto him. "I vow to honor and cherish you. To do good and not harm unto you all the days of your life. To care for you and love you in both sickness and in health, for all of the days of my life until in death we part."

The words washed over him, and he'd not realized until then how much hearing this brave, fierce woman speak vows of her own meant to him. He lifted her hand to his lips, unable to keep from pressing a kiss there.

Father Ivan cleared his throat, though the humor flickering in his eyes belied any annoyance at his lord and lady altering the ceremony. He proceeded to offer a short homily on the sacred act of marriage, though Robert hardly listened. Finally, they both knelt as the priest spoke a blessing over them. When he finished, he raised a joyous shout.

"Your lord and lady!"

At Father Ivan's pronouncement, the people cheered.

Robert helped Avery back to her feet and gathered her hands in his, pulling her close. "This day I have been greatly blessed." He reached down and captured her chin, pressing a gentle kiss to her perfect lips.

Avery's heart felt near to bursting. She stood on the dais in the grand hall of a massive castle, wife to a baron and lady of Northwood. She'd started her journey a few weeks before, thinking to spend one last vacation on the road. See a few sights, relive a few memories. Instead, her entire world had changed. Part of her wondered what the people back home would think when she never returned to work.

Would Mrs. Easley put out a missing person's alert

for her? Considering the woman seemed to know more about all of this time-warp stuff than Avery, probably not. But would anyone come looking for her? Involve the police? She had no control over any of that, and they were all questions that didn't matter, not to her, not here. She'd been given a second chance. A new beginning and the start of a life filled with love.

For that, she would forever be thankful.

Avery had been given a castle for Christmas. How many people got to say that?

"Thank you for the thoughtful gift, Wife." Robert leaned the shield against the wall behind the table, his smile infectious. "I will carry it with great honor."

"I am most pleased it suits, Husband." Avery took her groom's hand, satisfaction and contentment filling her as he welcomed the people to eat and make merry. She closed her eyes and offered up a simple prayer of thanks.

For a new life. For love. And for the joy of Christmas miracles.

Epilogue

Mrs. Easley slid the dusting rag over the dresser in slow circles, humming "Silent Night." She waited, hoping. Would she get an answer to her prayer? Just as she finished the final circle with the rag, a strange light began to twinkle, filling the tower room with a golden glow. Her breath caught. She dropped the rag and hurried to the gilded frame hanging on the wall.

The light faded, dipping the old room into shadows once more. Mrs. Easley smiled, running her fingers over the names displayed behind the glass. An answer.

In small script, the old ancestry chart held the names she sought. Sir Robert de Northwood, married to Lady Avery de Gardenia, foreign princess. Five little lines formed beneath the names, indicating five children. Three boys and two girls. From there, the lines diverged, listing an entire family that had loved and lived in Northwood Castle for seven more generations. Mrs. Easley lovingly followed the history. More names flowed down the page, coming finally to rest at the last two at the bottom.

Her name, beside that of Harold Easley.

She ran a finger across the two lines that symbolized her own marriage. "When the work is done, my love. Then we'll see each other again." She gave the frame a fond pat and turned away.

With a contented smile, Mrs. Easley threw the rag over her shoulder. Another mission successfully completed. She had to hurry now. The next guests would be checking in soon, and she didn't want to miss getting their room ready. Just as she was about to step through the door, something caught her attention. An object she'd not noticed earlier.

A small wooden box she'd not seen before sat on the writing desk. The aged hinges groaned as Mrs. Easley gently lifted the lid.

Inside, a delicate golden band encrusted with a rectangular sapphire and a wreath of diamonds and amethysts nestled against a tiny velvet pillow. Mrs. Easley lifted the ring and examined the ancient object. Beautiful. She slid it on her finger, surprised to see that it fit perfectly.

Next to the box lay a small embossed card with clean, perfect handwriting.

It read simply: *Merry Christmas.*

Dear reader,

I hope you enjoyed Avery and Sir Robert's story. If you would take a few moments to leave a review online, I would truly appreciate it!

Don't miss the next book in The Back Inn Time Series!

Coming Soon!

Check out the series page for the latest new additions.

Looking for even more time travel? Check out Her Place in Time!

Books by Stephenia H. McGee

Ironwood Plantation
The Whistle Walk
Heir of Hope
Missing Mercy
*Ironwood Series Set
*Get the entire series at a discounted price

The Accidental Spy Series
*Previously published as The Liberator Series
An Accidental Spy
A Dangerous Performance
A Daring Pursuit
*Accidental Spy Series Set
*Get the entire series at a discounted price

Stand Alone Historical Titles
In His Eyes
Eternity Between Us

Contemporary
The Cedar Key

Time Travel
Her Place in Time
(Stand alone, but ties to Rosswood from The Accidental Spy
Series)
The Hope of Christmas Past
(Stand alone, but ties to Belmont from In His Eyes)
The Back Inn Time Series

Novellas
The Heart of Home
The Hope of Christmas Past

www.StepheniaMcGee.com
Sign up for my newsletter to be the first to see new
cover reveals and be notified of release dates
New newsletter subscribers receive a free book!
Get yours here
bookhip.com/QCZVKZ

About the Author

Award winning author of Christian historical novels, Stephenia H. McGee writes stories of faith, hope, and healing set in the Deep South. She's a homeschool mom of two boys, writer, dreamer, and husband spoiler. Stephenia lives in Mississippi with her sons, handsome hubby, and their fur babies.

Visit her website at www.StepheniaMcGee.com and be sure to sign up for the newsletter to get sneak peeks, behind the scenes fun, the occasional recipe, and special giveaways.

Facebook: Stephenia H. McGee, Christian Fiction Author

Twitter: @StepheniaHMcGee

Instagram: stepheniahmcgee

Pinterest: Stephenia H. McGee